craved

(book #10 in the vampire journals)

morgan rice

ISBN: **978-1-939416-52-0**

Books by Morgan Rice

THE SORCERER'S RING
A QUEST OF HEROES (BOOK #1)
A MARCH OF KINGS (BOOK #2)
A FEAST OF DRAGONS (BOOK #3)
A CLASH OF HONOR (BOOK #4)
A VOW OF GLORY (BOOK #5)
A CHARGE OF VALOR (BOOK #6)
A RITE OF SWORDS (BOOK #7)
A GRANT OF ARMS (BOOK #8)
A SKY OF SPELLS (BOOK #9)
A SEA OF SHIELDS (BOOK #10)
A REIGN OF STEEL (BOOK #11)

THE SURVIVAL TRILOGY
ARENA ONE (Book #1)
ARENA TWO (Book #2)

the Vampire Journals
turned (book #1)
loved (book #2)
betrayed (book #3)
destined (book #4)
desired (book #5)
betrothed (book #6)
vowed (book #7)
found (book #8)
resurrected (book #9)
craved (book #10)

"O blessed, blessed night! I am afeard.
Being in night, all this is but a dream,
Too flattering-sweet to be substantial."

—William Shakespeare, *Romeo and Juliet*

CHAPTER ONE

Caitlin Paine sped down the West Side Highway, determined to reach the Cloisters before they closed. Her mind spun, as she reflected on all the troubles that were besieging Scarlet—troubles that no teenager should have. Scarlet was changing, Caitlin was sure of it. She was no mere human anymore, and each day, she was getting worse. Caitlin sensed that she was becoming what she, Caitlin, had once been herself: a vampire.

Of course, Caitlin had no direct memory of being a vampire herself; but from what she'd read in that journal she'd discovered in the attic—her vampire journal—she felt that it was all real. If the journal was true, and she sensed that it was, then at one time she had been one herself, back in time; somehow, she had ended up back here, in the present, with a normal life, a normal family, and no memory of it.

The only thing was, her family was far from normal. Her life was far from normal. Her daughter, somehow, was becoming what she had once been herself.

Caitlin wished, for the millionth time, that she had never found that journal. She felt that finding it was like opening Pandora's box, was what had sparked this parade of nightmares. She wished desperately that she could just make everything go back to normal.

She had to have answers. She had to know for sure that this was all authentic. If she couldn't force things back to normal, then she had to at least find out more about what was happening to Scarlet. And find out if there was any way to fix it.

As she drove, Caitlin thought again of the rare books she had found in her library. Most of all, she that of that one rare volume, and its torn page. She thought of its ancient ceremony, the one in Latin, with its cure for vampirism. She wondered again if it was real. Was that just passed down from folklore? An old wives' tale?

Any serious scholar, of course, would say that it was. And a part of her wanted to dismiss it, too. But another part of her was clinging to it, clinging to this last possible hope to save Scarlet. For the millionth time, she wondered how she could ever find the other half of that page. It came from one of the most rare books in existence, and even if she could somehow manage to track down another existing copy, what were the chances of the other half of the page being inside? After all, the page had been torn out, likely as a way of hiding it. But from who? From what? The mystery only deepened in her mind.

She tried to focus instead on her own journal, her own handwriting from centuries ago, on her description of the vampire coven beneath the Cloisters. She had written of a secret chamber leading to the coven, down below, on a lower level. She had to know if it was real. If there was some sign, any sign at all, then it would validate all of this in her mind, would allow her to confidently go forth. But if there was no sign here, then it discredited her entire journal.

Caitlin got off the highway, wound through Fort Tryon Park, and drove into the main entrance of the Cloisters. She drove up a narrow, winding ramp, and finally parked before the massive structure.

As she got out, she stopped and looked up; for some odd reason, the place felt strikingly familiar to her, as if it had been an important place in her life. She could not understand why, because as far as she knew, she had only visited it once or twice. Unless, of course, everything in her vampire journal was true. Was what she was feeling real? Or was it all just wishful thinking?

She hurried through the arched front door, into the stone medieval structure, up a long ramp, and down a long, narrow corridor. She finally got to the main entrance, paid a fee, and headed down a corridor. She passed a small courtyard on her right with rows of stone arches, inside of which sat a medieval garden. The fall foliage shimmered. It was a weekday afternoon, and the place was nearly empty, and she felt as if she had all to herself.

That is, until she heard music. At first, it was just a voice—then several voices. Singing. Ancient singing from a small chorus. She could not fathom if it was live or a recording as she stood there, transfixed, listening to the heavenly voices echo throughout the small castle. She felt transported, as if she'd arrived in another place and time.

She knew she had a mission to accomplish, but she had to see where the music was coming from. She turned down another corridor and followed the sound. She entered through a small, arched medieval door, and found herself in a chapel, with soaring ceilings and stained-glass. Standing there, to her surprise, was a chorus of six singers, older men and women, dressed in all white robes. They faced an empty room, looking down at sheet music as they sang out.

Gregorian chants. Caitlin saw the sign, the huge poster advertising the afternoon concert. She realized she had stumbled into a live performance. Yet, she was the only one in the room. Apparently, no one else knew about it.

Caitlin closed her eyes as she listened to the music. It was so beautiful, so haunting, she found it hard to leave. She opened her eyes and looked around at the medieval walls and furniture, and it made her feel even more out of touch with reality. Where was she?

The song finally ended, and she turned and hurried from the room, trying to regain her sense of reality.

She hurried back down the corridor and came to a stone staircase. She descended, winding down to the lower levels of the cloisters, and as she did, her heart beat faster. This place felt so eerily familiar, as if she'd spent time here before. She could not understand it.

She hurried across the lower level, remembering its description from an entry in her journals. She remembered the mention of the doorway, the secret portal, that led downstairs to a subterranean level, to Caleb's coven.

She got more excited as she saw, on her left, a roped off area. Behind the rope was a perfectly preserved, medieval staircase. It led up, but only into the ceiling. It didn't go anywhere. It was just an artifact, on display. The same one described in her journal.

But the staircase also had a small, wooden gate hiding the lower half, and behind it, Caitlin could not tell if the steps led down, to another level. It was roped off, and she couldn't get anywhere near it.

She had to know. If it led down, then everything she wrote about was true, not just a fantasy.

She looked both ways and spotted a security guard on the far side of the room, nodding off.

She knew that by crossing the rope in a museum she could get in big trouble—maybe even get arrested. But she had to know. She had to do this quick.

Caitlin suddenly stepped over the velvet rope, towards the staircase.

Immediately, an alarm went off, shrieking, piercing through the air.

"HEY LADY!" the guard screamed.

He started to run towards her. The alarm was piercing, and her heart pounded in her chest.

But it was too late now. She couldn't turn back. She *had* to know. It went against everything in her nature to step over that rope, to violate a museum display, to do anything against the rules—especially where history and artifacts were concerned. But she had no choice. Scarlet's life was at stake.

Caitlin reached the staircase and grabbed the medieval wooden handle. She yanked on it.

The gate opened, and as it did, she saw where the staircase led.

Nowhere. It ended at the floor. It was a fake staircase. Just a display.

Her heart sank, devastated. There was no subterranean chamber. No trapdoor. Nothing. As the display indicated, it was just a staircase. In and of itself. An artifact. An old relic. It was all a lie. All of it.

Caitlin suddenly felt rough arms grab her from behind and drag her out, up over the velvet rope, onto the other side.

"What do you think you're doing!?" another guard yelled, as he came over and helped drag her away.

"I'm sorry," she said, trying to think quick. "I…um…I lost my earing. It fell out, and it bounced on the floor. I thought it went over there. I was just looking for it."

"This is a museum, lady!" he barked, red-faced. "You can't just cross lines like that. And you can't touch things!"

"I'm so sorry," she said, her throat dry. She prayed they didn't arrest her. They certainly could, she knew.

The two guards looked at each other, as if debating.

Finally, one said, "Get out of here!"

He shoved her, and Caitlin, relieved, took off, hurrying down the corridor. She spotted an open door, heading outside, to a lower terrace, and she ran through it.

She found herself outside, on the lower terrace, in the cool October air, her heart still pounding. She was so happy to be out of there. Yet at the same time, she was distraught. There was nothing here. Was her entire journal made up? Was none of this real? Was she imagining everything?

But then how would that explain Aiden's reaction?

Caitlin crossed the cobblestone terrace, passing another medieval garden, this one filled with small fruit trees. She kept walking until she came to a marble railing. She leaned against it and looked out; in the distance she could see the Hudson River, sparkling in the late afternoon sun.

She suddenly turned, expecting for some reason to see Caleb standing there, beside her. For some reason, she felt she'd been here before, stood here on this terrace with Caleb. It didn't make any sense. Was she losing her mind?

Now, she was not so sure.

CHAPTER TWO

Scarlet burst into her room, hysterically crying, and slammed the door behind her. She'd run all the way home, from the river, and had not stopped crying since. She didn't understand what was happening to her. That moment kept flashing in her mind when she saw the pulse in Blake's neck, when she felt that feeling, that urge, of wanting to bite him. Of wanting to feed.

What was happening to her? Was she some kind of freak? Why had she felt that way? And why then—of all moments? Just as they were having their first kiss?

Now that she was far away from the scene, it was harder for Scarlet to summon exactly how her body felt at the time—and with each passing moment, it was growing more distant. Her body felt normal now. Had it just been a fleeting moment? Was it just some weird, one-time thing that had overcome her, that would never come back again?

She desperately wanted to believe that. But another part of her, a deeper part, felt that wasn't the case. The feeling had been so strong, it had been something she would never forget. If she had succumbed to it, and stayed there one more second, she felt certain Blake would be dead right now.

Scarlet couldn't help but think back to the other day. Coming home sick. Running out of the house. Forgetting what had happened, where she had been. Waking up in the hospital. Her mom being so worried, so freaked out….

Now, it all came to the forefront of her mind. Her mom had wanted her to see more doctors, to get more tests. And then, to see a priest. Did her mom suspect something? Was that what she was hinting at? Did she think that she was becoming a vampire?

Scarlet's heart was pounding as she sat there, in her room, curled up in her favorite chair. Ruth stuck her head in her lap, and Scarlet leaned down and stroked her. But there were tears in her eyes as she did. She felt shell-shocked, in a daze. She was terrified at the idea that she was sick, that she had some kind of disease—or maybe, something worse. Deep down she thought it was ridiculous, of course, where her mind was going. But she dared to wonder. Her wanting to bite his neck. The feeling she'd had in her two incisor teeth. Her craving to feed. Was it possible?

Was she a vampire?

Did vampires really exist?

She reached over, opened her laptop, and googled it. She had to know.

She pulled up the Wikipedia entry for "vampire" and began to read:

"The notion of vampirism has existed for millennia; cultures such as the Mesopotamians, Hebrews, Ancient Greeks, and Romans had tales of demons and spirits which are considered precursors to modern vampires. However, despite the occurrence of vampire-like creatures in these ancient civilizations, the folklore for the entity we know today as the vampire originates almost exclusively from early 18th-century southeastern Europe, when verbal traditions of many ethnic groups of the region were recorded and published. In most cases, vampires are revenants of evil beings, suicide victims, or witches, but they can also be created by a malevolent spirit possessing a corpse or by being bitten by a vampire."

Scarlet quickly shut her laptop and put it away. It was all too much for her to take.

She shook her head, trying to physically put it out of her mind. Something was definitely wrong with her. But was it that? It terrified her.

Making all of this even worse were her feelings for Blake, and her thinking of what had just happened between them. She couldn't believe she had run away from him like that, especially at that moment. They had been having such an amazing time, a dream date. And now this. Finally, just when their relationship was starting to take off. It was so unfair.

She couldn't even imagine what he was thinking right now. He must be thinking she's some kind of freak, some kind of absolute psycho, for her to just jump up like that, in the middle of a kiss, and take off, sprinting into the woods. He must think she was totally out of her mind. She was sure he'd never want to see her again. He'd probably go back to Vivian.

She desperately wanted to explain herself. But how could she possibly? What could she possibly say? That she had a sudden urge to bite his neck? To feed on him? To drink his blood? That she had to run away to protect him?

Sure, that would really set his mind at ease, she thought.

She wanted to make things right. She wanted to see him again. But she had no idea how to explain. Not only that, but she was also afraid to be near him; she didn't trust herself now. What if the urge overcame her again? And what if, next time, she actually hurt him?

She burst into tears, thinking about it. Was she doomed to never be around boys again?

No. She had to try. She had to at least *try* to make things right. She had to try to explain herself, in some way. If for no other reason so that he didn't hate her. Even if he never wanted to see her again, she couldn't just leave things like this. And deep down, a part of her still dared to hope that maybe this was just a one-time thing, a freak episode, and that maybe they could get over this and still be together. After all, if they could get over this, they could get over anything.

Scarlet was beginning to feel a little better. She wiped away her tears, grabbed a tissue, blew her nose, and took out her cell. She pulled up his number and began to text him.

Then she stopped. What should she say?

I'm so sorry for what happened today.

She deleted that. It was too generic.

I don't know what came over me today.

She deleted that, too. It didn't sound quite right. She needed the perfect balance, the perfect mixture of apologizing and yet being hopeful that things had not changed forever. She also needed to emphasize what a great time she had up until that point.

She closed her eyes and sighed, thinking hard. *Come on, come on*, she willed herself.

She began to type.

I had such an amazing time with you today. I'm so sorry it ended the way it did. There was a reason I had to leave like that, but I can't explain it to you. I know it's hard to understand, but I hope you can. I just want you to know that I had an awesome time, and I'm sorry. And I hope we can see each other again.

Scarlet stared at her draft for a long while, then finally reached out, and hit send.

She watched it go through.

Her text wasn't perfect. She already thought of how she could have re-written it in a million ways. And a part of her already regretted sending it. Maybe it sounded too desperate. Maybe it was too cryptic.

Whatever. It was off. At least now he knew that she still liked him, and that she wanted to see him again.

She knew that Blake had his cell on him every second of the day. She knew he'd get it right away. And that he always answered his texts within seconds.

Scarlet trembled as she waited to hear.

She placed her cell on her lap and closed her eyes, breathing slowly, waiting for a vibration. Willing it to vibrate.

Come on, she thought. *Text me back.*

She sat there, waiting, for what felt like forever. She kept refreshing her phone. After a few minutes, she even powered it off then back on, in case somehow it was jammed. She then watched the clock tick. Two minutes passed.

Then five.

Then ten.

She slammed her phone down on the table, and could feel tears welling up inside again. He clearly wasn't texting her back. How could she blame him? She probably wouldn't text herself back either.

So that was it. It was over.

Then, suddenly, her phone vibrated.

She reached over and snatched it off the table.

But her heart fell to see that it wasn't Blake. It was Maria.

I can't believe u cut class like that. So…how was ur date with Blake?

Scarlet sighed. She had no idea how to respond.

Don't worry. I'm not cutting again. It's over between us.

Really? OMG. Why? Vivian?

No. Not her. It just…

Scarlet stopped, wondering what to say.

…didn't work out.

Tell me.

Scarlet sighed. She really wanted to change the subject.

Nothing to tell. What's up with u?

OMG, I can't stop obsessing about new boy. Sage. Heard fresh details today.

Scarlet was exhausted and really didn't want to continue this texting conversation. She didn't want to hear more gossip and innuendo about the new kid—or about anyone. She just wanted to disappear from the world.

But Maria was her best friend, so she had to humor her:

Like what?

He has a sister, and a cousin. They don't go to our school though. He's a senior. He transferred from a private school. I hear he's rich. Like super-rich.

Scarlet didn't care. She just wanted to end this.

Luckily, before she could type, she got another text—this one from Jasmin.

OMG, what's happening to your Facebook wall?

Scarlet read it in surprise.

What do u mean?

Before she could respond, she grabbed her laptop, opened it, and pulled up her wall.

Her heart plummeted. Vivian had posted on it:

Nice try stealing Blake. It didn't work. After he dumped you, he came back to us. I knew he'd dump you. Just surprised it happened so soon.

Scarlet breathed sharply, completely taken aback. She saw various friends of hers comment on the post, and saw that it had spread to many people's walls. She also saw that Vivian had posted it to Twitter, and that it had been re-tweeted by all of Vivian's friends.

Scarlet was aghast. She had never felt more embarrassed. She deleted the comment from her wall, blocked Vivian, then went to her settings and changed them so that only her friends could post. But it was barely a drop in the bucket—clearly, the damage had already been done. Now the whole school thought that she was stealing other people's boyfriends. And that she was dumped.

Her face turned red. She was so mad, she wanted to reach out and strangle Vivian. She didn't know what to do.

She slammed down her laptop, and burst out of her room. She tore down the steps, not knowing where to go or what to do. All she knew was that she needed air.

"Come on Ruth," she said.

She grabbed her leash and Ruth jumped excitedly, following her out the door and down the porch steps.

Scarlet ran down the steps, looking at her feet, and it wasn't until she was out on the sidewalk that she looked up, and saw him, standing there.

She stopped cold.

He stood there, staring back at her, as if he was waiting.

It was the new boy.

Sage.

CHAPTER THREE

Scarlet stood there, at the end of her walkway, staring. She could hardly believe it. There, standing on the sidewalk, just a few feet away, staring back with his intense grey eyes, was the new boy. Sage.

What was he doing here, in front of her house? How long had he been standing here? Had he been watching her house? Had he been about to head up her walkway? Or had he just been passing by?

But passing by where? She lived on a quiet suburban street, and hardly anyone ever walked around here. Then again, she was only two blocks to town, and conceivably, he could be heading somewhere. But that was unlikely.

The thought of him standing there, watching her house, or about to walk up, freaked her out. On the other hand, she couldn't deny that she was excited to see him. Excited wasn't the right word. It was more like…transfixed. She could not take her eyes off of him. His smooth skin, his strong jaw, his proud cheekbones and nose, his gray eyes, long eyelashes—she had never met anyone remotely like him. So noble, so proud. He seemed so out of place here, like he'd dropped down out of a sixteenth-century palace.

She also couldn't help noticing that she felt butterflies in her stomach when she looked at him. And it was a feeling she did not want to have. After all, Maria, her best friend, had made it clear that she was obsessed with him. How wrong would it be for Scarlet to take him away? Maria would never forgive her. And she would never forgive herself. Besides, she had Blake. Or did she?

She thought again of Vivian's post, about Blake dumping her. Had Blake really told her that? Or had Vivian made it up? Either way, she felt pretty sure that Blake was gone from her life for good.

"Um…hi," she said, not knowing what else to say. After all, they had never even been introduced.

"I didn't mean to startle you," he said back.

She loved his voice. It was soft, gentle, yet powerful the same time. He was soft-spoken, yet there were something authoritative in his tone. She could listen to that voice forever.

"I'm Sage," he said, extending a hand.

"I know," she said, as she reached out and took it.

The touch of his skin was electrifying. It sent a thrill up her harm, as he held her freezing hand in his warm one.

"Small town," she added, by way of explanation, but then felt embarrassed. That was stupid of her; she shouldn't have admitted she knew his name. It made her seem desperate.

But wait, she thought. Why was she even thinking this way? After all, he was Maria's man. Wasn't he?

"Your hand is so cold," he said, as he looked down at her palm.

Scarlet withdrew it, self-conscious.

"Sorry," she said, shrugging.

"You didn't tell me your name," he said.

"Oh, sorry, I just figured you knew it," she said, then added, "not that I'm famous or popular anything. It's just…well, small town, you know?"

She was already stumbling, making things worse with each sentence. She always did this when she got nervous in front of guys.

"Anyway, my name is Scarlet. Scarlet Paine."

He smiled.

"Scarlet," he echoed.

She loved the sound of her name in his voice.

"The color of many things. Wine, or blood, or roses. Of course, I prefer the latter," he added with a smile.

Scarlet smiled back. Who talked like this? she wondered. It was as if he were from another time, another place. She was dying to know more about him.

"What are you doing here?" she asked, then figured that sounded too harsh. "Not to be rude or anything. But I mean like, what are you doing in front of my house?"

He momentarily looked flustered.

"Yes," he said. "Peculiar timing, isn't it? I was just in town, and thought I'd do a bit of exploring. I'm new here, and thought I would see where these roads lead. I had no idea they led to you."

Scarlet felt better. At least he wasn't stalking her house or anything.

"Well, there's not much to see. This town is only a few blocks in each direction. A few more blocks that way, and it's done."

He smiled. "Yes. I was beginning to see that myself."

Suddenly, Ruth ran up to him and jumped up and licked his hand.

"Don't jump," Scarlet chided.

"It's okay," he said.

He knelt down, and petted Ruth gently, stroking her mane with his palm, scratching behind her ears. Ruth leaned in and licked him on the cheek. She started whining and Scarlet could tell that she really liked him. She was shocked. Ruth was always so protective of her, and she'd never seen her take to a stranger like this.

"What a beautiful animal. Aren't you, Ruth?" he said.

Ruth leaned up and licked him again, and he kissed her on the nose.

Scarlet was stunned.

"How did you know her name was Ruth?"

He suddenly stood, caught off guard.

"Um…I read it. On her neck tag."

"But the tag is faded," she said. "I mean, I can barely read it."

He shrugged, smiled.

"They always told me I had good vision," he said.

But Scarlet was not convinced. The tag was faded down to almost nothing, and she couldn't possibly see how he could have read it. It freaked her out. How did he know her name?

Yet, at the same time, she felt comfortable being around him. And given the state she was in, she liked having company. She didn't want him to go. But at the same time, she thought of Maria, and how upset she would be if she drove by and saw her standing here with him. She would be so jealous. She would probably hate her for life.

"You're quite the mystery around here," Scarlet said. "The new kid. No one really knows much about you. But a lot of people are dying to."

"Are they?" he shrugged.

Scarlet waited, but he didn't offer anything more.

"So…like…what's your story?" she asked.

"I guess everyone has one, don't they?" he asked.

He turned and looked off at the horizon, as if debating whether to tell her.

"I guess mine is boring," he said. "My family…recently relocated here. So here I am, finishing out my final year."

"I heard you had like…a sister?"

A smile formed at the corner of his mouth.

"Word gets around here, doesn't it?" he asked with a grin.

Scarlet blushed. "Sorry," she said.

"Yes, I do have one," he answered, but didn't offer any more.

"Sorry, didn't mean to pry," she said.

He looked at her, and as she looked up her eyes locked with his—and for a moment, she felt her world beginning to melt. For the first time that day, all her worries drifted far from her mind. She felt transported.

She wanted to stop staring, to put her feelings in check, wanted to summon thoughts of Maria and force herself to push him out of her mind. But she couldn't. She was frozen.

"I'm flattered that you did," he said.

He continued staring, then after a moment, he added, "Would you like to take a walk with me?"

Her heart started to pound. She *did* want to walk with him. She wanted that more than anything in the world. But a part of her was scared. She was still reeling from her time with Blake. She still didn't trust herself, her own feelings, her body, her reactions. And she was scared to betray her best friend—even if, in reality, Maria had no claim on Sage. Most of all, she didn't trust herself. Whatever had happened between her and Blake, that impulse to feed, might still be there. As much as she wanted to know more, she felt the need to protect him.

"I'm sorry," she said. "I can't."

She saw disappointment in his eyes as he nodded back. "I understand."

Scarlet suddenly heard the banging of doors inside her house, along with the muted sound of voices rising. It was her parents, arguing. She could hear it even from here. Another door slammed, and she turned and looked to the house with concern.

"I'm sorry, but I have to go back inside now—" she said, as she turned back to say her goodbyes.

But as she turned back, she was utterly confounded. There was no sign of Sage. Anywhere.

She looked both ways, turned up and down the block, but there was nothing. It was unfathomable. It was as if he'd just vanished.

She wondered how he could have possibly run away that quickly. It was impossible.

She wondered where he went, and if there was still time to catch up to him. Because now, she felt an overwhelming urge to be with him, to talk to him. She realized, in a flash, that she had just made the stupidest mistake of her life by saying no. Now that he was gone, every ounce of her ached for him. She'd been such a fool. She hated herself.

Had she lost her chance for good?

CHAPTER FOUR

Still shaken from her encounter with Sage, Scarlet walked into her house lost in her own world.

She was snapped out of it rudely as she walked right into the middle of her parents' arguing. She couldn't believe it. In all her life, she never remembered them arguing and now that was all they did; she felt a pang of guilt, wondering if it had to do with her. She couldn't help shake the feeling that something bad had started in all of their lives, something that wouldn't go away, and which seemed to be escalating, day by day. And she couldn't help feeling as if it were all her fault.

"You're taking this way too far," Caleb screamed at Caitlin behind the closed door. "Seriously. What's gotten into you?"

"What's gotten into *you*?" Caitlin shot back. "You were always in my corner, always took my side. Now, it's like you're in denial."

"Denial?" he shot back.

Scarlet couldn't take it anymore. As if her day wasn't bad enough—having to listen to this was putting her over the edge. She just wanted them to stop arguing. She just wanted their lives to go back to normal.

She took a few steps in and pushed open the door to the dining room, hoping her presence would make them stop.

They both stopped in mid-argument, as they wheeled and stared at her, like deer caught in headlights.

"Where were you?" her dad snapped at her.

Scarlet was taken aback: her dad had never yelled at her before, and had never used that kind of tone. His face was still read from arguing, and she barely recognized him.

"What do you mean?" she said, defensive. "I was just outside, with Ruth."

"For an hour?"

"What are you talking about?" she said, wondering. "I was only outside for a few minutes."

"No you weren't. I went up and checked your room, then I saw you going outside, and that was an hour ago. Where did you go?" he insisted, walking around the table towards her. "Don't you lie to me."

Scarlet felt as if he'd totally lost his mind. Not only was her mom going crazy, her dad was, too. She felt her world caving in.

"I don't know what you're talking about," she snapped back, her own voice rising. But she was starting to wonder if somehow she'd lost track of time. If something was happening to her. If she had again gone somewhere, and not remembered. The thought of it made her heart pound, as she started to silently freak out. "I'm not lying. And I don't appreciate your accusing me of it."

"Do you have any idea how worried sick we were about you? I was about to call the police again."

"I'm sorry!" she yelled back. "I didn't do anything!"

She was shaking inside at the brunt of his anger, and couldn't stand it a moment longer. She turned and stormed out of the room, bursting into tears as she did. She ran up the steps.

She'd had it with her parents. It was just too much. Now, even her dad didn't understand her. And he had always, her whole life, been on her side, through everything.

"Scarlet, get back here!" he shouted.

"NO!" she screamed back, through her tears.

She could hear her dad's footsteps, following her up the steps, and she went faster. She hurried down the hall, to her room, and slammed the door behind her.

A moment later, his fist banged on the door.

"Scarlet. Open the door. I'm sorry. I want to talk to. Please. I'm sorry."

But Scarlet turned off the lights and jumped into bed, curling up. She sat there, crying and crying.

"Go away!" she screamed.

Finally, after what felt like forever, she heard his footsteps disappear.

It was too early to sleep, and Scarlet felt too numb to do anything else. After a long while, she reached over and picked up her phone. Her alerts were going crazy—her Facebook page blowing up with new posts and messages. It just made her feel worse, and she shut it off.

After a long while, she lay there, on her side, looking out through the window at the trees, at all the different colors, shimmering in the final light of day. She watched as several leaves fell off the trees before her eyes, swirling down to the ground.

She felt overwhelmed with sadness. Blake didn't want to be with her; Vivian had turned the whole school against her; her own friends didn't understand her; her parents didn't trust her; she didn't know what was happening to her body. And most of all, she messed up her chance to talk to Sage. Everything was going so wrong. And she couldn't stop flashing back to that moment between her and Blake, down by the river. She couldn't stop thinking about what was happening to her. Who was she, really?

She reached over and grabbed her journal and her favorite pen, leaned over and began to write.

I don't understand my life anymore. It's surreal. I just met the most amazing boy ever. Sage. I don't want to admit it, because Maria likes him, but I can't stop thinking about him. I feel like I've known him somehow. We barely spoke, yet I felt such a connection to him. Even more than with Blake.

But he left so quickly, and I stupidly turned him down. I wish I hadn't. There are so many questions I'm dying to ask him. Like who he is. What he's doing here. And why he was in front of my house. He said he was just walking by, but somehow I don't believe it. I think he was looking for me.

I don't know who my parents are anymore. Every day, everything is changing so much. I don't know who I am either. It's like the whole world I once knew, the world that was so familiar and safe is gone, replaced by another world. And I feel like tomorrow, it will all just change again.

I dread tomorrow. Will everybody hate me? Will Blake ignore me? Will I see Sage?

I can't even imagine what the next day will bring.

*

Scarlet opened her eyes, awakened by a doorbell. She looked out and was shocked to realize it was already late morning, the sun flooding into her bedroom. She realized she'd fallen asleep in her clothes, on top of the covers. She grabbed her clock and turned it: 8:30. Her heart fluttered with panic. She was late for school.

The doorbell rang again, and Scarlet jumped to her feet. Given the time, she assumed her parents had already left for work, so she

25

had to answer the door. Who could be ringing it so early in the morning?

She was tempted to ignore it, to just hurry up and get ready for school, but it rang again.

Ruth barked and barked and finally, Scarlet let her out and followed her down the stairs, through the living room, and towards the door.

Ruth stood before it, barking like crazy.

"Ruth!"

Finally Ruth quieted as Scarlet walked to the door. She slowly pulled it open.

Her heart stopped.

Standing there, staring back at her, was Sage. He held a long black rose, in both hands.

"I'm sorry to drop by like this," he said. "But I knew you'd be home."

"How?" she asked, totally confused.

He only stared back.

"May I come in?" he asked.

"Um…" Scarlet began.

A part of her desperately wanted to invite him in, but another part felt freaked out. What was he doing here? Why was he bringing her a black rose?

But then again, she couldn't just send him away.

"Sure," she said. "Come in."

Sage smiled wide, as he took a single big step across the threshold.

As he did, to her amazement, suddenly he sank into the floor. He sank and sank, as if into quicksand, and held up a hand, shrieking for her.

"Scarlet!" he shrieked. "Help me!"

Scarlet reached down and grabbed his hand, trying to pull him up. But she suddenly went down the hole, too, diving down face first. She screamed at the top of her lungs, as she went flying full speed, heading towards the bowels of the earth.

Scarlet woke screaming. She looked all around her room, her heart pounding. The first rays of the day came through her window. She looked over at her clock. 6:15.

She had fallen asleep in her clothes. She breathed hard as she realized it had all just been a dream.

Her heart was pounding. It had felt so real.

She got up, headed into her bathroom and splashed cold water on her face several times, trying to wake up. As she stared back into the mirror, though, her fears were compounded: her reflection. It was different. She was there, but her reflection was translucent, as if she were a ghost. As if she were fading away. At first she thought the light was playing tricks on her. But she turned up the light, and it was still the same.

She was so freaked out, she felt like crying. She didn't know what to do. She needed something to ground her. Someone to talk to. Someone to tell her that it would be OK. That she wasn't going crazy. That she wasn't changing. That she was the same old Scarlet.

For some reason, Scarlet thought of her mom's offer, of the priest. Now, she felt like she really needed him. Maybe he could help her feel better.

She walked out into the hall and as she did, saw her mom walking down the hall, getting dressed for work.

"Mom?" she asked.

Caitlin stopped and turned, looking surprised.

"Oh honey, I didn't know you were awake so early," she said. "Are you okay?"

Scarlet nodded, afraid she would cry, and walked down the hall and gave her mom a hug.

Her mom hugged her back, tightly, and rocked her, and it felt so good to be in her arms.

"I miss you honey," her mom said. "And I love you very much."

"I love you too," Scarlet said over her shoulder, and began to tear up.

"What's wrong?" her mom asked, as she pulled back.

Scarlet wiped a tear out of the corner of her eye.

"Do you remember your offer the other day? To see the priest?"

She nodded back.

"I'd like to go. Can we go together? After school today?"

Her mom smiled wide, seeming relieved.

"Of course we can, sweetheart."

She gave Scarlet another hug. "I love you. Don't ever forget that."

"I love you too, mom."

CHAPTER FIVE

Scarlet got to school early, for the first time in ages. The halls hadn't filled up yet, and it was a ghost town as she walked to her locker. She was used to coming in late, to the place being packed, but today, after her nightmare, she felt too antsy to sit around the house and wait. She'd also checked her Facebook and Twitter and saw the ridiculous amount of activity as a result of Vivian and her friends posting about her, and was so anxious about how the school might react, she felt coming in early might somehow help fend it off. At least by getting here early, she felt somewhat grounded, somewhat prepared.

Although of course she knew that would do no good. Soon these halls would fill with an overwhelming number of kids, and they would cluster in groups, outnumber her, and look and whisper. Including, maybe, Blake. She wondered what he might have told everyone about their date. Did he tell them everything that happened? Did he tell them that she was some kind of freak?

The thought of it made her so sick, she'd skipped breakfast this morning. She would have to face the music, and wondered how many hundreds of kids had been following the posts—and what they all thought about her. A part of her wanted to curl up and die, to run away and leave this town, and never come back.

But she knew neither of these were an option, so she figured, better to just be brave and get it over with.

As she opened her locker and collected her books for the day, she realized how far behind she was in all her homework assignments. This, too, was so unlike her. The last two days had been so crazy, everything so different than it had ever been. Making matters worse, she was squinting at the morning light coming in through the windows, and noticed she had a terrible headache she'd never had before. She found herself shielding her eyes at a particularly bright hallway, and wondered again if something was wrong with her. Was she still sick or something?

She spotted her old sunglasses sitting up there, on the top shelf of her locker, and felt like grabbing them and wearing them indoors, throughout the day. But she knew that would only attract more negative attention.

Like a tidal wave, the halls began to fill with kids, pouring in from every direction. She glanced at her phone and realized her first class would start in a few minutes. She took a deep breath and closed her locker.

She'd noticed on her phone that there were no new texts, and her thoughts turned again to Blake, to yesterday. Her running away. She wondered again what he must have told the others. Had he really said all those harmful things? That he'd dumped her? Or had Vivian made them up? What did he really think of her? And why hadn't he answered any of her texts?

She assumed, of course, that his silence was a response. That he was freaked out, and no longer interested. But she wished, at least, that he'd respond, as she checked her phone yet again, just in case— even if just to say he wasn't interested. She hated not hearing.

As if all that were not enough, she could not stop thinking about Sage, either. Their meeting, in front of her house, had been so mysterious. She regretted walking away from him, and wished she had a few more moments to talk to him, to ask him more questions. Her dream freaked her out, though, and she could not understand why he was stuck in her mind, even more so than Blake.

She felt so confused. With Blake, it was like she consciously thought about him; with Sage, it was like she couldn't help it—she thought about him whether she wanted to or not, and she didn't understand her strong feelings for him. Strangely enough, even though she'd known Blake for years, she already somehow felt closer to Sage. What bothered her more than anything was that it didn't make sense. She hated not understanding—especially when it came to love.

"Oh my God, Scarlet?" came the voice.

As she closed her locker she saw Maria standing there, looking back at her as if she were looking at an infamous celebrity.

"You're never here early! I texted you like a million times last night! What happened? Where were you? Are you OK?"

Scarlet felt a pang of regret; she'd been too overwhelmed to reply to all her texts. She also felt a new feeling of nervousness around Maria, given her feelings for Sage. After all, Maria made it clear that she was obsessed with Sage. If she found out Scarlet had talked to him the night before—especially in front of her own house—she feared Maria would freak out. Maria was so possessive and territorial when it came to boys. She always thought that whoever she laid her eyes on was hers—whether the person knew of her existence or not. And if anyone even remotely got in the way, they were her instant enemy. She could be very spiteful like that—and she would never forgive and forget. She was that kind of person: either your closest friend, or your mortal enemy.

"Sorry," Scarlet replied. "I crashed early. I wasn't feeling well. And I couldn't deal with the whole Facebook thing."

"OMG, I hate her," Maria said. "Vivian. What a snake. Who does she think she is? I posted on her wall, and on her friends' walls, too. I put them all in their place for bashing you."

Scarlet felt so appreciative towards Maria—which made her feel even more guilty for having talked to Sage. She wished she could just tell her, just explain to her what happened with Sage—but she didn't really understand herself what had happened. And she feared that if she even mentioned it, Maria would lose it.

"You're the best," Scarlet said, as she put an arm around her in appreciation.

The two of them walked side-by-side, down the halls, which were quickly filling up, the noise getting louder and louder, as they began the long march down towards the other end of school, for their first class together.

"I mean, the nerve of her," Maria said. "First, stealing your man. Then, posting all about it. She's just threatened. And jealous. She just knows you're the better girl."

Scarlet felt a little bit better, yet still felt a twinge of sadness at the idea of losing Blake. Especially under these circumstances. All she wanted was a chance to explain to Blake, to tell him that, whatever happened down at the river, that wasn't her. But she didn't really know how to explain. What could she say to him? She guessed she'd laid it out well enough in her text. And he never even replied.

"Hey guys," came the voice.

Walking up beside them were Jasmin and Becca. Scarlet sensed them looking her over, and was beginning to feel paranoid about all the attention.

"Hey," Scarlet said, as they all walked together, heading as a small group down the halls. "So are you going to like keep us in suspense?" Jasmin asked. "What happened with Blake?"

Scarlet could feel the eyes on her, and felt flustered. As they walked, she also saw the glances of all the kids. She wanted to think that she was just being paranoid—but she knew she wasn't. There were definitely a ton of people looking at her, stealing side glances, as if she were some kind of freak. She wondered again how many kids had been online, had read all the posts, and what they believed. Was she going to be known as the girl who got dumped by Blake? Who lost Blake to Vivian? She burned at the thought of it.

"Is it true?" Becca asked. "Did he really dump you?"

"If he did," Jasmin said, "just tell us, and we'll slam his Facebook wall."

"Thanks guys," Scarlet said. She thought about how to best respond. She didn't really know how to explain.

"So?" Maria prodded. "Are you really not going to tell us?"

Scarlet shrugged.

"I'm not sure what to say. There really is nothing to tell. We went down to the river, and like…" She paused, debating how to phrase it. "…Blake kissed me."

"And?" Jasmin prodded. "You're killing us here!"

Scarlet shrugged.

"That's it. Nothing really happened. I mean, I like him. I still do like him. But…I left. I mean, I started feeling like really sick, so I had to leave, kind of abruptly."

"What do you mean sick?" Becca asked.

"Like my stomach started killing me," she lied, not knowing what else to say. "And I had this really bad headache." At least it was partially true, she thought. "I think I was just still sick from the other day. So I rushed out of there. Bad timing, I guess."

"So did Blake like bring you back? Or was he like a total jerk?" Jasmin asked.

Scarlet shrugged.

"It's not his fault. I didn't really give him time to, I guess. I kind of just left. I felt bad about it. I wanted to explain it to him. But he never answered my text."

"What a jerk," Maria said.

"What a loser," Jasmin added. "Seriously. So you got sick—so what, he doesn't answer your texts? What's his problem? So you were sick. Big deal. I mean like he's not going give you a chance to explain?"

"Totally," Maria chimed in. "And then, what, he goes running back to Vivian, and like dumps you for her? Just because you were sick? What's his problem? He totally doesn't deserve you. It's for the best."

Scarlet really appreciated all the voices of support, and it made her feel better. She had never thought of it that way. She guessed she had been her own worst critic. The more she thought about it, the more she realized they had a point. Maybe Blake should have been more sympathetic; maybe he should have followed up, asked her how she was feeling; maybe he shouldn't have been so quick to run to Vivian.

But had he really? Or had Vivian made it up?

"Thanks guys," she said. "I really appreciate it. Though honestly I don't really know what happened after. I don't know if he went back to Vivian or if she just made it all up."

"So I guess that means you're not going with him to the dance?" Maria asked. "So then who are you going with? I mean, are you like not going?" she asked, her voice rising as if that were the most horrible thing in the world.

Scarlet shrugged. That stupid dance—it couldn't have come at a worse time. She really didn't know what to say.

"I doubt Blake's taking me," she said. "As far as going alone…."

For a moment, Scarlet couldn't help but think of Sage. She realized how much she'd actually like to go with him. She hardly knew why. His face just stuck in her mind.

At the same time, she thought of Maria, what she would think— and the thought of going with Sage felt like a betrayal. She quickly tried to push it out of her mind.

"If I don't go, I don't go," she finally said. "It's okay. Maybe next year."

"There's a huge pre-game party tonight at Jake Wilson's house. His parents are away. We're all going. You *have* to go. Maybe you'll find a date there."

Scarlet gulped. Sneaking out and searching for a date tonight was the last thing she wanted to do.

"Well anyway don't feel bad," Maria said. "I don't have a date yet either."

"What about Brian?" Jasmin asked her.

"We're over, remember?" she said.

"But he's not dating anyone else."

Maria shrugged. "He didn't ask me. And I really wouldn't want to go with him anyway. Sage is the one I really want to go with. The new boy."

Scarlet gulped.

"So why don't you ask him?" Becca asked.

"Yeah, you keep talking about him, but you're not doing anything about it," Jasmin said. "Stop being chicken."

"I'm not chicken," Maria snapped back.

"Chicken chicken!" they taunted her.

Maria's face turned beet red, and Scarlet could see how mad she was.

"I'm not chicken. In fact, I have class with him next period. I'm going to ask him then."

"No you're not," Becca said.

"You'd never do that," Jasmin said.

"Watch me," Maria said.

"But isn't that like awkward?" Becca said. "Your asking him?"

Maria shrugged. "It could be better. But what am I supposed to do? He's new. If I don't ask him, somebody else will. And if he's not into me, I'd rather know now, right?"

"I still think you're all talk," Jasmin said.

Maria glared at her. "Check back in an hour and we'll see who's all talk."

Scarlet was relieved that the conversation had shifted away from her. She was beginning to feel hopeful, as if maybe all the negative attention would actually pass over quickly, and not be as bad as she thought. After all, kids moved on to new topics of gossip really quickly. But as she thought of next period's class, with Sage and Maria, her stomach sank.

As they rounded the corner, Scarlet's stomach sank further: there, huddled against a wall, were Vivian and her friends. They elbowed each other, looking in her direction, then giggled and whispered.

Vivian turned and glared right at her with a victorious smile. She could see the meanness in her perfect face, the petty vindication she received from having bullied her online. For a moment, Scarlet was so mad, she felt like attacking her. She felt a tremendous rage rush through her, tingling, running up from her toes through her fingertips. She didn't understand what was happening: it was like a hot flash. Her body felt stronger, more violent, and less able to control itself. She wanted to get out of here quick, before anything bad happened.

"Well well well," Vivian said aloud, as they all walked past. The tension in the air was so thick, it could be cut with a knife.

"Look who it is. If it isn't Blake's leftovers."

"That's quite a statement, especially coming from Blake's reject," Jasmin snapped back at her.

"What are you too afraid to say it to her face, so you have to go and post it online?" Maria goaded.

Vivian's face dropped into a scowl, as did her friends. Scarlet was mortified. She just wanted all of this to pass away. She appreciated her friends' loyalty, but she didn't want this to evolve into a full-fledged war.

"And this coming from a girl who doesn't even have a date to the dance," Vivian retorted, as she now homed in on Maria. "Loser," she said.

"I'd rather not have a date then have someone's leftovers," Maria snapped back.

"Please Maria," Scarlet said quietly. "Let's just keep going."

For a moment, it felt as if the two groups of girls would lunge at each other, and that this would evolve into a full-fledged fight. As much rage as Scarlet felt coursing through her, she really didn't want any more confrontation.

She gently prodded her friends and slowly her group kept walking, going farther down the hall. Scarlet did not want to descend to Vivian's level.

Just as the two groups were gaining more distance between each other, suddenly Scarlet sensed something. It was a strange sensation, one she'd never had before. Out of nowhere, her senses were on high alert: she felt, more than saw, a dark energy approaching her from behind. She didn't know how, but she did. And then her hearing became so much acute: she heard every tiny movement in the hallway. She heard the movement of a girl's footsteps, approaching her from behind.

Reacting at the speed of light, Scarlet suddenly felt her body turn itself around, felt her own hand go up as she spun, and watched herself grab someone else's hand just as it approached the back of her head.

Scarlet looked up and was amazed to see herself clutching Vivian's wrist. She looked over and saw a big wad of chewing gum in her palm, and saw her shocked expression. Then she realized what had happened: Vivian had crept up behind her and was about to cram the gum into her hair. Somehow, Scarlet had sensed it and had spun and blocked it at the last second, just inches away.

As Scarlet stood there, she found herself twisting Vivian's wrist with an incredible surge of strength; Vivian dropped down to her knees, and screamed out in pain.

Everyone in the halls stopped, as a huge crowd gathered around.

"You're hurting me!" Vivian cried out. "Let go!"

"FIGHT! FIGHT!" screamed the crowd of kids who suddenly gathered around.

Scarlet felt an overwhelming rage coursing through her, a rage she could barely control. Something in her body had protected her from getting hurt, and now it was willing her to get vengeance—to break this girl's wrist.

"Why should she?" Maria yelled out. "You were about to stick gum in her hair."

"Please!" Vivian whimpered. "I'm sorry!"

Scarlet didn't understand what was overcoming her, and it freaked her out. Somehow, at the last second, she willed herself to stop. She finally let go.

Vivian's wrist collapsed to her side, as she scrambled to her feet and ran back to her group of friends.

Scarlet turned, her heart pounding, and walked with her friends back down the hall. Slowly, the halls came back to life again, everyone whispering, as they dispersed. Scarlet's friends clustered around her.

"OMG, like how did you do that?" Maria asked, in awe.

"That was like amazing!" Jasmin said. "You really put her in her place."

"I can't believe she was about to gum you," Becca said.

"She got what she deserved," Maria said. "Nice going, girl. I think she'll think twice about messing with you again."

But Scarlet didn't feel good. She just felt empty, drained. And more bewildered than ever about what was happening to her. On the one hand, of course she was thrilled she was able to catch her in time, to fight back and stand up for herself. But at the same time, she couldn't understand how she'd been able to react the way she had.

Her eyes were hurting even more and her headache was worsening, and as crazy as it sounded, she couldn't help feeling as if she were changing somehow. And that terrified her more than anything.

The bell rang, and just before they headed to class, Scarlet looked over and saw Blake standing there. He stood with a few of his friends, and one of them prodded him, and he turned and glanced at her. For a moment, their eyes locked. Scarlet tried to decode his expression. She hoped more than anything that he would turn and walk over to her, give her a chance.

But he suddenly turned and walked with his friends in the opposite direction.

Scarlet felt her heart breaking. So that was it. He wasn't into her anymore. Not only that, but he wasn't even talking to her. He wouldn't even acknowledge her. That hurt her more than anything. She'd thought they had something real together, and couldn't understand how it had all fallen apart so quickly, how he could walk away so easily. How he couldn't at least be more understanding of her—at least have given her a chance to explain.

It wasn't even the first period of the day and already Scarlet felt beat up, like a punching bag. She'd already experienced a whirlwind of emotions, and wondered how she'd be able to make it through the day.

"Come on, you don't need him," Maria said, as she wrapped an arm around Scarlet's, and guided her into the day's first class. Scarlet gulped, knowing that waiting behind those doors was Sage.

CHAPTER SIX

Scarlet's first period class was filled with about thirty kids, everyone scrambling to take their seats. The desks were lined up single file in three neat rows of ten, while to the side of the room were long wooden tables, benches beneath them. She scanned the room and saw with relief that Sage wasn't in it; at least that was one less drama to deal with today.

"Where is he?" Maria asked, dejected. "Figures."

It was English, Scarlet's favorite class. Normally, she'd be happy to be here, especially because Mr. Sparrow was her favorite teacher, and especially because this term they were studying Shakespeare and her favorite play: *Romeo and Juliet*.

But as she slumped into her seat, in the row next to Maria, she felt deflated. Apathetic. She could hardly concentrate on Shakespeare. The class quieted, and she took out her books by rote and stared at the page, in a daze.

"Today's going to be a little different," Mr. Sparrow announced.

Scarlet looked up, happy to hear the sound of his voice. In his late 30s, good-looking, slightly unshaven, with longish hair and a strong jaw, he looked out of place in this high school. He looked a bit more glamorous than the others, like an actor slightly past his prime. He was always so happy, so quick to smile, and so kind to her—and to all the students. He never had a harsh word for her, or for anyone, and he always gave everyone As. He also managed to make even the most complicated text easy to understand, and actually managed to get everyone excited about whatever they were reading. He was also one of the smartest people she'd ever met—with an encyclopedic knowledge of world and classic literature.

"It's one thing to just read Shakespeare's plays," he announced, a mischievous smile on his face. "It's quite another to act them," he added. "In fact, one could argue that you can't truly gain an understanding of his plays until you've read them aloud yourself—and even tried to act them."

The class giggled in response, the kids looking and murmuring at each other in an excited buzz.

"That's right," he said. "You guessed it. After today's discussion, we're going to break off into groups, each of you choosing a partner and act the text aloud to each other."

Excited whispers spread in the classroom, and the energy level definitely rose a few notches. It managed to shake Scarlet from her reverie, managed to make her forget, for a few moments, all the troubles in her life. Partnering up and reading the lines: that would definitely be fun.

Suddenly, the door to the room opened, and Scarlet turned, with the rest of the class, to see who it was.

She could not believe it. Standing there, proudly, book in his hand, was Sage, wearing a slim leather jacket, black leather boots and designer jeans with a large black leather belt and huge silver buckle. He wore a black button-down shirt hanging loose, and it revealed sparkling necklace—it looked like white platinum—with a large pendant in the middle. It looked like it was made of rubies and sapphires, and sparkled the light.

Mr. Sparrow turned and looked at him, surprised.

"And you are?"

"Sage," he replied, handing him a slip. "Sorry I'm late. I'm new."

"Well then you are most welcome," Mr. Sparrow responded. "Please class, welcome Sage and make room for him in the back."

Mr. Sparrow turned back to the chalkboard.

"Romeo and Juliet. To begin with, let's talk about the background of this play...."

Mr. Sparrow's voice faded out in Scarlet's head. Her heart pounded as Sage walked down the rows of seats. And then suddenly, she realized: the only empty seat in the room was directly behind her.

Oh no, she thought. *Not with Maria sitting right next to her.*

As Sage walked down the aisle, she could have sworn she saw him turn and stare right at her. She looked away quickly, thinking of Maria, and not understanding why he was looking at her like that.

She felt more than saw him walk behind her, heard his chair scrape and felt him take a seat behind her. She could feel the energy coming off of him; it was tremendous.

Suddenly, her phone buzzed in her pocket. She furtively reached down, slipped it out a couple inches, and looked. Of course. Maria.

OMG, I'm dying.

Scarlet pushed her cell back into her pocket, and didn't turn and look at Maria, not wanting to make it obvious they were texting. She then put her hands back on her desk, hoping Maria would just stop texting. She really didn't want to text now. She wanted to concentrate.

But her phone buzzed again. She couldn't ignore it, especially with Maria sitting right next to her, so again, she reached down.

Hello? What should I do?

Again, Scarlet pushed her cell back into her pocket. She didn't want to be rude, but she had no idea what to say and really didn't want to get into a texting conversation right now. The situation was just getting worse, and she wanted to focus on what Mr. Sparrow was saying, especially as they were on her favorite play.

But then again, she couldn't completely ignore Maria. She quickly reached down and typed with one finger.

Don't know.

She hit send, then pushed her cell deep into her pocket, hoping Maria would leave her alone.

"Romeo and Juliet," Mr. Sparrow began, "was not an original story. Shakespeare actually based it on an ancient tale. Like all of Shakespeare's plays, he found his sources in history. He recycled old stories and adapted them into his own language, in his own time. We like to think that he's the greatest original writer of all time—but in truth, it would be more accurate to call him the greatest *adapter* of all time. If here were alive and writing today, he would not win the award for best Original Screenplay—he would win for best *Adapted* Screenplay. Because none of his stories—not one—were original. They had all been written before, some many times over many centuries.

"But that doesn't necessarily detract from his great skill, from his ability as a writer. After all, it's all about how you turn a phrase, isn't it? The same plot told two ways can be boring in one instance and compelling in another, can't it? Shakespeare's great skill was his ability to take someone else's story and re-write it in his own words, for his own time. And to write it with such beauty and poetry that he really brought it to life for the first time. He was a dramatist, yes. But ultimately, and most of all, he was a poet."

Mr. Sparrow paused as he lifted the play.

"In the case of *Romeo and Juliet*, the story had already been around for centuries by the time Shakespeare got his hands on it. Does anyone know the original source?"

Mr. Sparrow looked around the class, and it was dead silent. He waited several seconds, then opened his mouth to speak—when suddenly, he stopped and looked right in Scarlet's direction.

Scarlet's heart pounded as she thought he was looking at her.

"Ah, the new boy," Mr. Sparrow asked. "Please enlighten us."

The entire class turned and looked in Scarlet's direction, at Sage. She was relieved to realize he wasn't calling on her.

She couldn't help turning just a bit, too, looking behind her, at Sage. Instead of looking at the teacher, oddly, Sage looked at her as he spoke.

"Romeo and Juliet was based on a poem by Arthur Brooke: *The Tragicall Historye of Romeus and Iuliet.*"

"Very good!" Mr. Sparrow said, sounding impressed. "And for extra points, might you know the year it was written?"

Scarlet was amazed. How had Sage known that?

"1562," Sage replied, without hesitating.

Mr. Jordan looked happily surprised.

"Amazing! I've never had any student get that. Bravo, Sage. Since you're such a scholar, here's one final question. I've never known anyone—even among my peers—to get this right, so don't feel badly if you don't. If you get it, I'll start you off with an automatic 100 on your first test. Where and when was the play first performed?"

The entire class turned in their seats and looked at Sage, the tension running high. Scarlet looked, too, and saw Sage smile back at her.

"It is believed to have been first performed in 1593, at a small venue called The Theatre, on the opposite side of the Thames."

Mr. Jordan shouted out in excitement.

"WOW! My Sage, you are good. Wow, I'm impressed."

Sage cleared his throat, not finished.

"That is the common understanding," Sage said, "but in truth, it was actually performed once before that. In 1592. In Elizabeth's castle. In her courtyard, amidst her private orchard."

Scarlet looked back at Sage, speechless. His eyes had a far-off look, almost as if he were remembering being there himself. She couldn't understand.

Mr. Sparrow's smile fell.

"Oh, you were doing so good, Sage. I'm sorry. I'm afraid you are mistaken there. You should have quit while you were ahead—you actually had it right the first time. It was never performed before 1593."

"Actually, I'm sorry sir, but I am correct," Sage insisted gently but firmly.

Mr. Sparrow looked back at him, eyes opening wide in amazement.

"And what is your source?" he asked.

There was a long pause, as Sage sat there, apparently thinking. Scarlet was amazed. *Who was this kid?*

"I have none," he said finally.

Slowly, Mr. Sparrow shook his head.

"I'm afraid without a source, we can't verify, can we? I'll tell you what: find me the source, and I'll gladly reinstate your 100.

"In the meantime class," Mr. Sparrow continued, "it's time to break off into partners. Please find one, proceed to the benches, and open to Act one, Scene Five."

There was a loud shuffling in the room, as everybody rose and headed over to the long benches on the side of the room.

"Remember, it's a boy-girl scene!" Mr. Sparrow yelled out. "I want girls partnered with boys, and vice versa!"

Scarlet was about to partner up with Maria until he made this announcement, throwing her off.

"OMG, what should I do?" Maria whispered as she hurried over. Maria, flushed, was staring at Sage, who was just getting up.

"This is my chance," Maria said. "I have to partner with him."

"Go for it," Scarlet said, half-heartedly. She wanted Maria to be happy, but she couldn't help it: another part of her wanted to partner with Sage herself.

Scarlet headed over to the long, wide benches on the far side of the room and took a seat alone at the far end, beneath a window, all alone. She unfolded her book before her. Since she wasn't going to partner with Sage, she didn't really care who she partnered with: she didn't like any of the boys in this class. She figured she'd just sit there and wait for one of them to come up to her, because she didn't really feel like seeking one of them out.

She looked up and watched Maria approach Sage. Maria went right over to him, and was the first to reach him; Scarlet noticed other girls trying to get to him, too, but Maria was first. She had her chance.

Sage turned and glanced at Maria, and Maria stepped forward. She opened her mouth to speak, but then stopped. She froze up.

"Hi," Maria said to him, apparently too scared to say anything else.

"Hi," he said back.

He waited a few seconds, but Maria stood there, opening and closing her mouth a few times. Finally, she turned away, her face red.

Scarlet could not believe it. Maria turned and headed in her direction, and as she did, two other girls walked up to Sage.

But Sage turned his back on them, and instead looked right at Scarlet. To Scarlet's horror, he bee lined right for her.

She looked down, burying her head in the play. A part of her willed him to talk to her. But another part willed for him not to; it would be a like a slap in the face to Maria.

Oh my god, she thought. *I can't believe this is happening to me. Why here? Why now?*

She looked up as he took a seat on the bench opposite her, facing her across the wooden table. He smiled as he stared at her.

"Is this seat taken?" he asked.

Scarlet turned red, not knowing what to do. She shook her head and looked back down, hoping that Maria wasn't watching this.

"You can sit wherever you want," she said.

"What I was really asking was if you would be my partner?" he continued.

Scarlet looked up. She could hardly ignore him at this point. Now Maria was standing beside her, looking down, watching. She could see in Maria's eyes that she was desperate, silently begging her to say no.

"Actually," Scarlet said, wanting to be a loyal friend, despite her own feelings for Sage, "I think you'd be a really perfect partner for my friend, Maria."

As she said it, Scarlet got up, slid out of her seat, grabbed Maria, and slid her into the seat she had just been in.

She saw Maria flustered, but happy, break into a big smile, as she reached out an awkward hand.

"I'm Maria," she said to Sage.

Sage, clearly not wanting to be rude, reached out and shook her hand, and Maria shook his way too hard, awkwardly, smiling like an idiot.

"I know," he said. "I just heard. Pleased to meet you."

Scarlet sat beside Maria, feeling sad but good that she had been as loyal as can be. As she did, a boy sat opposite her.

Oh no, she thought. *Not him.*

Spencer. He was a geeky kid, covered in acne, his shirt buttoned up to his neck. He smiled at her, revealing a mouth full of braces.

"Hey Scarlet," he said with a lisp.

He was nice enough, though Scarlet was not remotely attracted to him. But she didn't want to hurt his feelings.

"Hi Spencer," she said matter-of-factly.

"So like I guess we're partners, huh?" he said, proudly.

"I guess so," Scarlet replied.

Scarlet sat there, burning up inside, hoping that Maria appreciated the supreme sacrifice she had just made for her.

As she sat there, out of the corner of her eyes, she could not help but notice Sage. Oddly, he wasn't looking at Maria, but rather looking diagonally, directly at Scarlet. His staring at her was obvious, and Scarlet was flustered. Clearly, Maria would see this, and she knew it would upset her.

"So did you like hear about this big dance tomorrow night?" Maria asked Sage.

Scarlet watched his reaction. He was expressionless, clearly not wanting to engage Maria.

"I did," he said back to her, leaving it at that.

Scarlet wondered if Maria would have the courage to follow up, to flat-out ask him if he wanted to go with her. But an awkward silence followed.

She heard Maria swallow; clearly, she was too nervous to ask him.

"Okay class!" Mr. Sparrow yelled out. "Boys, you of course are Romeo and girls, Juliet. In this scene, Romeo and Juliet are in a lavish costume ball. They see each other for the first time. It is love at first sight. And although they don't know each other, in their first words, they express their undying love for one another. Clearly, we are not going to re-enact the dance in this room."

The class erupted into a giggle.

"But," he continued, "try to read the lines with meaning. Feel how it feels to be Romeo, feel how it feels to be Juliet. Feel how the language feels when you pronounce it aloud. What is the difference between pronouncing it aloud and reading it to yourself? This will take us to the end of class. Feel free to begin."

A chorus of voices erupted around them, as everyone began reading.

"O, she doth teach the torches to burn bright! It seems she hangs upon the cheek of night like a rich jewel in an Ethiope's ear..." Spencer began to read to Scarlet.

His voice was so nasally, and his pronouncement so stiff, she had to suppress a smile. It was possibly the worst reading she had ever heard, and the farthest thing from romantic she had ever encountered—it sounded robotic, as if a computer had recited the line. She bit her lip, forcing herself not to smile, not wanting to embarrass him.

She read her lines back to him quickly, without any expression of meaning.

Scarlet stole a glance over at Sage, and as she did, she saw him staring right at her.

"Did my heart love till now? forswear it, sight! For I ne'er saw true beauty till this night," he read, right to her, with perfect intonation and the deepest meaning.

There was no mistaking it: he was staring at her when he said it.

Scarlet's heart raced. She glanced over at Maria, wondering if she'd seen it. Luckily, Maria, nervous, had her head buried in her book, looking down, too nervous to look up at Sage. She hadn't seen it. But Scarlet had. Sage was reading his lines to her. Scarlet.

"Saints have hands that pilgrims' hands do touch, and palm to palm is holy palmers' kiss," Scarlet read. She couldn't help it: as she read the lines, she found herself looking back at Sage, reading them to him.

"That's not the line you're supposed to read!" Spencer corrected loudly. "You're reading the wrong line!"

Scarlet looked over at him, her face turning red. What a pest. He was beyond annoying, and ruining her moment.

"My lips, two blushing pilgrims, ready stand to smooth that rough touch with a tender kiss," Sage read. Again, as he read it, he stared right at Scarlet.

This time, Maria looked up, and saw. She realized that Sage was not looking at her, but at Scarlet. And as she did, her face turned red with anger.

The bell rang, and suddenly everyone rose from their seats. Maria grabbed her book, stuffed it into her backpack, and stormed past Scarlet.

"I thought you were my friend," Maria hissed at her as she passed.

Scarlet was so flustered, she hardly knew what to do, or how to respond. She went to talk to her, but Maria was already gone, storming out the room. If possible, Scarlet felt even worse now than ever.

"Hey Scarlet, that was like really cool!" came the nasally, chipper voice.

She looked over to see Spencer standing way too close to her, grinning, his braces in her face, and his breath smelling like Salami. "We should like hang out more often!"

He stood there, grinning, leaning in even closer until he was just inches away—and Scarlet finally turned her head away, revolted. She conspicuously bent over and gathered her books, and finally, to her relief, Spencer disappeared.

Scarlet was even madder, wondering if Spencer had now also managed to scare Sage away.

But then suddenly she heard a voice—a soft, gentle, mature voice.

"Your friend is upset," Sage said.

Scarlet looked up and saw with relief that he was still there.

"But you did nothing wrong. I never wanted to be with her. I want to be with you."

Scarlet stopped as she looked into his eyes. As she did, she felt her whole world melting. She had been thinking the same exact thing.

"I'm sorry," Scarlet said, breathless. "But she's my friend. And she likes you."

"But she's not the one I like," Sage replied.

Scarlet was overwhelmed with the desire to ask him why. Why did he like her? How was he so sure? How was all of this possible? Especially when they didn't even know each other?

She desperately wanted talk to him, to ask him questions, to stand there and be with him. She didn't want to leave this room.

But it was all too much for her. She was overwhelmed with conflicting emotions, and she couldn't help feeling disloyal to Maria for even talking to him.

So despite every bone in her body, she turned and hurried from the room, out the door and into the never-ending stream of kids, feeling her heart tearing into a million little pieces.

CHAPTER SEVEN

Scarlet walked with her mom down the cobblestone pathway to the church's front door, feeling self-conscious. She had never been to church before, even though it was just two blocks from her house, and she didn't want any of her friends to see her walking up to it now. The church was so conspicuous, right on main street in the middle of town; she lowered her baseball cap, which she'd snatched off the coat rack at the last second, hoping nobody saw her. It wasn't that she thought there was anything wrong with going to church—it was just that it just wasn't her. It wasn't her family. She thought it would be weird for some of her friends or neighbors to suddenly see her walking with her mom to church in the middle of the day. After all, why would anyone do that? Unless something was wrong with the family.

But she knew that going to church would make her mom happy, and for some weird reason, she sort of looked forward to it, too, given how unsettled she was feeling these days. She wouldn't mind actually having someone to talk to, assuming this priest was cool, which her mom said he was, and not some strict, old guy. She doubted that he could relate to her, but maybe he could help shed some light on what was wrong with her. Or maybe he could at least make her feel more calm.

As they walked, Scarlet reflected on her day. It had been another lousy one. After first period, everything was anti-climactic: she didn't see Sage again all day, even though she couldn't stop thinking about him. She wondered if he hated her now, for leaving like that. Despite herself, she hoped that he liked her. She looked for him all day, but saw no sign of him. It was so weird—it was like he disappeared.

At least thinking about him had taken the edge off of Blake. With Sage in her thoughts, she had hardly thought of Blake again that day; the one or two times she had seen him, out of the corner of her eye, she was sure that he had seen her too, and had quickly turned away. He definitely hadn't texted her all day. So it was obvious that he wasn't into her anymore. Which was starting to feel okay with her, as long as she thought of Sage.

Despite her efforts, she hadn't crossed paths with Maria again that day; she was sure that Maria was giving her the cold shoulder—and worse, she could have sworn that Jasmin and Becca were avoiding her, too. She wondered if Maria had told them what had happened and had cast Scarlet in a bad light. She hadn't seen any of them at lunch, which was unusual. Scarlet was increasingly feeling as if she had no one left to turn to. Her friends, Blake, her parents—she was feeling that everyone was aligned against her.

The final bell of the day had been a welcome sound and she'd hurried back home and checked her cell again, but had still received no texts from Maria, or any of her other friends. That was a sure sign. Maria was a chronic texter, as were the others. Clearly something was up. Maria had probably told them all Scarlet tried to steal her boyfriend—which was ridiculous, because Sage wasn't Maria's boyfriend, and because he didn't even like her. Not to mention that Maria didn't even have the guts to ask him, and that Scarlet had actually looked out for her by swapping partners. But still, obviously, in Maria's mind, that was what had happened.

Scarlet figured she should be the bigger person, and finally texted Maria after school, giving her her perspective of what had happened. But Maria didn't reply. It was so typical. Maria could be the most loyal friend in the world—but she could also be the most spiteful and territorial

Scarlet had finally had enough, and had put her phone away and powered it off. These days, it seemed to give her nothing but aggravation anyway. She'd waited eagerly for her mom to get home from work and now that it was almost sunset, she was actually looking forward to hearing what this priest had to say. Clearly, her life couldn't get any worse.

The heavy door to the church creaked open, and as they walked inside, Scarlet felt transported to another world. It was quiet and dark in here, and as she took in the smooth stone floors, the old, worn pews, the stained-glass windows, it gave her a sense of peace. She was surprised at how at-home she felt—and even more surprised that she had never been here before.

Suddenly, the church bells rang out, striking six o'clock. After the traditional bells, there followed a song, ringing out in chimes. It was the most beautiful thing Scarlet had ever heard, and she felt grateful to her mom.

"Thanks for bringing me," she said to her mom.

Her mom squeezed her hand as her face broke into a smile, and Scarlet felt guilty she had been so stubborn.

A side door opened at the far end of the church, and in came Father McMullen, wearing a welcoming smile.

"And you must be Scarlet," he said in a cheery voice, as he strutted towards them. He extended his hand way out in front of him, before he even reached them. Scarlet shook his hand, and he shook hers back, encasing it with both of his hands heartily.

"I've heard so many lovely things about you. Thank you for coming."

"Thanks for having me," she said, not knowing how to reply.

As he held her hands in his, he stared into her eyes, and as she looked up into his light blue eyes, she couldn't help but feel as if he were dissecting her. As if he sensed something that surprised him.

He quickly withdrew his two hands. As he did, his expression changed to one of hesitation—maybe even fear.

He cleared his throat.

"Please, come this way," he said as he turned and led them down the aisle.

They followed him down the long aisle, passing the pews, and as they did, Scarlet noticed him looking side to side, his expression increasingly worried. She turned to see what he was looking at, and noticed the rows of tall, burning candles: as they passed, one at a time, each candle burned out.

By the time they reached the end of the aisle, all the candles along the walls had been extinguished—and as they approached the altar, the dozens of small votive candles all suddenly blew out, too.

The Father stopped cold in his tracks. He stood there, his back to them, as if afraid to turn around.

Scarlet stared at the candles, not understanding what was happening. Had it been a draft? She hadn't felt one.

The Father slowly turned and looked at her. From his fearful expression, she couldn't help but wonder if maybe she were to blame.

She saw small beads of sweat form on his forehead, as his eyes travel down to her throat.

"That's a beautiful necklace," he said.

Scarlet detected a shakiness in his voice that wasn't there a moment before. Clearly, he was freaked out. He was freaked out by *her*, she realized. That scared her, and she started to tremble.

"May I ask where you got it?" he asked.

"I gave it to her," her mom chimed in. "For her sixteenth birthday. Just a few days ago."

He turned and looked at her.

"Where did *you* get it?" he asked, with intensity.

"It's been in my family for generations," she responded. "My grandmother gave it to me. And her grandmother gave it to her."

"May I look at it?" he asked, turning to Scarlet.

Scarlet nodded, not knowing what to say.

He reached out and gently lifted the cross with two fingers, staring at it in the light. As he did, his eyes widened in fear.

"The cross of the Resurrection," he whispered to himself, in terror.

"You know it?" her mom asked.

He let it go, pulling back his hand as if he'd touched a snake.

"Of course," he said. "It is said to trace back all the way to the times of Christ. It is one of the most famous crosses of Christianity. It was rumored to have been lost centuries ago. It is a holy relic. I can't understand how you have it. Something like this, it belongs in the Vatican. In a museum. On display."

Scarlet reached up and fingered the necklace, feeling a whole new appreciation for it. And a fear of it. Why was he so scared by it?

"That cross," he continued, "is rumored to have been used to protect the first vampires."

"Vampires?" Scarlet asked, heart pounding.

"What do you mean protect them?" her mom asked.

"In the early days of Christianity, the vampires were rumored to be the chosen ones. The good ones. When barbarians waged war against the holy people, it was the vampires, the super race, that was called to protect mankind. Back then, you see, it was a great blessing to be a vampire. It was somewhat like being a priest today. They were the chosen kind, and blessed with immortality.

"But somewhere along the way, it changed. One too many vampires were turned. An evil strain occurred among them. Over time, the evil strain became dominant, and wiped out the good ones. Only a handful of good ones remained throughout the centuries. And this cross was there symbol. They were the Knights Templar of vampires, their most elite sect.”

He suddenly turned to Caitlin.

“Your grandmother…who was she exactly?” he asked.

“Um…well…” she began, flustered.

Suddenly the sun shifted, its huge red ball aligning directly in the path of the stained-glass window, in the center of the far wall. It lit her up, sending a single beam of sunlight right to Scarlet. Light flooded her.

Scarlet suddenly felt a horrific pain, right in her forehead. It was so bad, she had to clutch her head. Her eyes burned, too, as if they were on fire. She keeled over. It felt like it was tearing her up inside, and she couldn’t stand it for another second.

She shrieked as she dropped to her knees, clutching her head.

“Make it stop! Make it stop!” she screamed.

“Scarlet what’s wrong?” her mom cried out, dropping to her side, putting an arm around her.

The priest took a step back, eyes widening in fear.

“*Sancte Michael Archangele, defende nos in proelio, contra nequitiam et insidias diaboli esto praesidium,*” he began to chant, raising a hand in the sign of the cross. He reached into his cloak, grabbed a small decanter of holy water, and sprinkled it on Scarlet.

As the water hit her skin, in the sunlight, it felt like acid. She shrieked.

But this time, it was no normal shriek. It was the guttural roar of animal, several octaves lower. It was a horrific noise, one that sent the hairs standing on the back of the human’s necks. She shrieked and shrieked, standing, throwing back her arms, sending her mom flying, crashing into the wooden pews.

The shriek grew so loud that the entire room began to shake; as it did, all the stained-glass, on every wall, shattered, exploding in every direction.

Father McMullen turned and fled, sprinting for all he had.

Scarlet threw back her head and roared. The roar rose higher and higher, louder than the sound of the bells, louder than the sound of the exploding glass, as fragments of every color showered down all around her.

CHAPTER EIGHT

Scarlet opened her eyes to see her mom looking down on her. She blinked several times, as she slowly came into focus. Her mom looked down in concern. On her other side her dad stood over her, too, also looking down with concern.

Scarlet looked around and realized she was lying in her bed, in her bedroom. She glanced out the window, and saw it was night, and looked over, and saw her clock blinked 9 PM. She wondered how she got here. She tried to piece it all together, but it was hazy. It freaked her out that her parents were in here. What were they doing here, in her bedroom, looking at her like that?

"Scarlet, are you okay honey?" her mom asked with concern.

Scarlet checked in with her body and realized she felt totally fine. She just couldn't figure out how she got here.

Scarlet sat up in bed.

"What happened?"

"Do you remember?" her mom asked. "The church?"

Church. Scarlet thought back, and started to remember. She recalled going to church with her mom, talking to that priest. She remembered the candles blowing out…remembered him talking about her necklace…and then….

Her mind went blank.

"What happened?" she asked.

Her mom looked down, as if debating how to phrase it.

"Well…" she began. "You passed out. And I carried you home, and put you to bed. That was three hours ago."

"Hi sweetheart," her dad chimed in, holding her hand. "I'm so glad to see you're doing okay."

Scarlet tried to remember passing out, but couldn't.

"I'm sorry," she said. "Maybe I had like low blood sugar or something. I've never fainted before."

"Did you skip lunch?" her dad asked.

Scarlet thought back. Yes, she had.

"Actually, I did. And breakfast, too…. It was a stressful day, and I kind of forgot."

"Well, then that explains it," her dad said, sounding confident and assured, as if ready to put this whole thing to rest. "You just needed to eat. Being in church probably stressed you out, and you fainted. No big deal. I'm glad you're okay now."

"Wait a minute," her mom said. "That's not all that happened."

"Why can't you just let things lie?" he snapped at her. "You're blowing this whole thing up to be more—"

"Guys, I'm right here," Scarlet snapped at them both, tired of their arguing. "I'm totally fine. Seriously. There's like nothing to worry about. I blacked out. I'm sorry. I guess I didn't eat or whatever."

Scarlet couldn't take their fighting anymore; she couldn't stand being around them. They both looked at her, momentarily silenced.

"Can we talk in private?" her dad asked her mom, sternly.

The two of them quickly shuffled out of the room, closing the door behind them, and immediately, Scarlet could hear the muffled sound of their arguing.

She held her hands to her ears and sighed. She hated it. Why did they have to argue all the time now? She couldn't help but feel as if it all had something to do with her, and it made her feel even worse.

She heard a loud buzzing and looked over and saw her phone light up on her nightstand table. She picked it up: a text from Maria.

Sorry was upset. Ur right. You didn't do anything. I guess I blew it out of proportion. Anyway, friends?

Scarlet smiled, feeling vindicated. Finally, something went right today. She typed:

Friends.

Her phone lit up immediately with another text from Maria:

Pre-game tonight?

Scarlet thought for a moment, not knowing what to say:

Not sure am up to it.

A part of her just wanted to curl up and go to sleep and forget this entire day. But another part of her actually liked the idea of getting out of the house, making up with Maria, distracting herself from this whole awful day.

Please. U have to come. need a wing man. I heard Sage will be there. this is my chance. and Blake will be there and heard he's in a fight with Vivian. Now is your chance.

The thought of entering that party, with Sage and Blake and Maria there—and Vivian and her friends there—put a pit in her stomach. But at the same time, she really wanted to reconcile with Maria and get out of the house. And despite herself, the thought of seeing Sage gave her a thrill.

Not sure.

Please. I'll be like the only single girl there. Need you.

Scarlet sighed. She thought hard. If she didn't go to the big dance tomorrow night—and it looked like she wasn't going—then at least she could have this night.

My parents would kill me, she texted back, already anticipating their reaction.

She waited a second, wondering if she should ask them. Of course not. Of course they would say no—especially after today. They were such worrywarts to begin with; they would never allow this.

But the more she thought about it, the more she realized: she really did want to go. In the back of her mind, she was hoping something might happen with Blake, or Sage. She was so confused, she wasn't even sure which one. But she wanted something to happen. She was tired of being alone.

Her phone lit up, and her heart fluttered as she read Maria's new text:

Sneak out.

Scarlet recoiled. She had never snuck out before.

But as she began to think about it, she actually started to wonder if it was a good idea. Why not? If she snuck out the window and got back in time, they'd never even know. She wasn't going to stay long anyway, and it was only a few blocks away.

Scarlet jumped up out of bed, Ruth tagging along, feeling a burst of energy and a fresh determination. She went to her door, opened it, let Ruth out, and listened. She could hear her parents arguing faintly, down the steps on the first floor. She made a decision. She stepped out into the hall and leaned over the bannister and screamed:

"I'm tired! I'm going to bed! Good night!"

She then slammed her door extra loud and locked it, not waiting for a response, hoping they wouldn't come and check on her.

She hurried through her room, refreshed her lipstick, brushed her hair, threw on fresh jeans, a light black sweater and a leather jacket, and turned off all the lights.

Then she crossed the room, opened her window, and slipped out onto the terrace. From there, it would be an easy climb down—she'd done it a million times.

Suddenly, she heard a banging on her bedroom door.

"Scarlet, open this door!" came the harsh voice. It was her dad.

One leg out the window, she hesitated, wondering if she should go back inside.

But as she stood there, debating, the fresh air felt good, and she really wanted to get away from all this. She realized she needed to change her environment; she couldn't stay in this house a minute longer.

She stepped out, closed the window behind her, and climbed down the trellis. In moments, she was in her backyard, trotting away, across their yard, across the street, and beginning her ten block walk to the party.

*

As Scarlet turned the corner, she was struck by all the activity on Jake's block, and in front of his house. All the other streets around here were dead quiet, with not a sign of life—but in stark contrast was Jake's block, lined with parked cars. His house was entirely lit up, every light on in every room on every floor, and dozens of kids on the front and back lawns, holding cups of beer and wine coolers. Music was blasting so loud that she could hear it even from here, a block away, along with the hum of conversation, shouts, laughter and partying.

There must be at least two hundred kids in that house, Scarlet thought.

She wondered how Jake was going to possibly clean all this up before his parents got home—and marveled that none of the neighbors in this super-quiet village had called the cops yet. She figured it was only a matter of time until they did.

Scarlet walked quickly, hugging her thin, fall coat tightly around her shoulders against the breeze as she approached. As she got closer and some kids looked in her direction, she felt a flutter in her stomach. There was so much drama behind those walls, it was kind of like going back to school all over again, except at night—and in a much more contained way.

56

As she reached the front walkway, she spotted Maria, standing there, arms wrapped around her shoulders trying to warm herself up, and waving Scarlet down with her cell. Her face lit up at the site of her.

"*There* you are!" she said, hurrying over to her, wrapping one arm around hers tightly and turning her, leading her up the walkway, side by side. "I've been waiting forever!"

"Why didn't you just go inside?" Scarlet asked.

"Are you kidding? Not so cool, to enter alone."

"Where are Jasmin and Becca?"

"Jasmin left already. Her boyfriend had other plans. Becca's inside, but she's with Jake."

The two of them walked past tons of kids, cups of beer in hand, several of them smoking; Scarlet watched one of them put his butt out, still smoking, into the hedges beside the house. She shook her head, hoping this house didn't catch on fire. As they walked past them, one of them blew smoke her way, and she could feel it seeping into her hair and clothes. *Great*, she thought. *Now her parents would smell it on her.*

They walked through the open door into the brightly-lit house, and inside, the activity hit Scarlet like a tidal wave. The music was cranking, the bass shaking the floors, and the rooms were packed shoulder to shoulder with kids dancing, laughing, singing, drinking from large red plastic cups, and spilling beer everywhere. She looked over and saw a small keg in the corner, and three of her classmates standing behind it, baseball caps turned backwards, filling rows of cups. The foam spilled out over the floor, onto the carpet, and no one seemed to care. The house already smelled like a frat party.

Lots of girls in her class held wine coolers, sipping from them; other girls held different cups, and Scarlet spotted them pouring from a small flask into cups of orange juice or lemonade. She could not believe how hard everyone was partying on a weeknight. Then again, the big dance was tomorrow, and under the watchful eyes of all the teachers, it wouldn't be as easy to get away with things. This, the pregame, was the real party.

"Come on!" Maria shouted over the music as she dragged her through room after room, and back into the kitchen area. "The wine coolers are back here."

The kitchen was far less crowded, with room to walk, and the music was more muted here, too. Scarlet followed Maria to a large metal bucket filled with ice, wine coolers floating inside. Maria reached down and grabbed two of them, not even asking Scarlet as she twisted opened hers and handed her one.

"Cheers," she said.

Scarlet hesitated; she rarely drank, and really didn't want to drink now. If her parents caught her sneaking back home, that would be bad enough; if they smelled alcohol on her, that would be the end of it.

But then again, Scarlet didn't want to seem like a pilgrim; so she figured she'd accept it, take a sip, then when no one was looking, set it down somewhere.

"Cheers," she said, clinking glasses and taking a sip; it went right to her head.

"I don't see him anywhere," Maria said.

"Who?" Scarlet asked.

"Sage. I heard it on good rumor that he's gonna be here. Have you seen him?"

Scarlet's stomach fluttered as she thought of him. She wanted more than anything to push thoughts of him out of her mind, to let him be completely Maria's. After all, Maria was her best friend, and she wanted her to be happy. But try as she did to suppress it, she couldn't help realizing she also felt something for Sage.

"No," she said back, nervously. "I haven't really been looking."

"So like what did he say to you after class?" Maria asked, turning to her. "Did he say anything about me? Does he like me?"

Scarlet could see how obsessed Maria was over him, could see that she wasn't letting it go. She had never seen her this bad before. Scarlet couldn't help wondering if Maria wanted to see her tonight to truly reconcile their friendship, or only because she wanted to get more information out of her about Sage.

Scarlet felt bad for her. She knew that what Sage had said—that he didn't like Maria—would devastate her. She didn't have the heart to tell her that. Besides, she could see that Maria was lost in her own fantasy, and that she wouldn't even believe it if she said it.

"He really didn't say anything. The bell rang, and I walked out."

"Do you think he was into our scene, when we were partnering up? I thought I saw him looking at you, and I got confused."

Scarlet didn't know how to reply. She really didn't want to let her friend down; but she couldn't lead her on, either.

"I really don't know. I don't know anything about him."

"But you were there. Tell me. What do you think? Was he into me?"

Scarlet had no idea what to say, so she just took another sip.

"OMG, I can't stop thinking about him," Maria continued, not waiting for a response. "I *have* to have him. I heard he still doesn't have a date for tomorrow night. I'm asking tonight. I decided. I really am this time. I'm going to force him to say yes."

"Hey guys," came the voice. They turned, and there stood Becca, arm in arm with her boyfriend, Jake. "Having fun?"

"Hey guys," Jake said.

"Hi Jake," they said. "Thanks for having us."

"You and the rest of the school," he laughed. "It's getting crazy."

"Are your parents gonna be pissed?" Maria asked.

He raised a finger to his mouth, as if to indicate silence.

"If my cleaning lady does her job, they'll never know. Let's just hope no one calls the cops."

They were suddenly grabbed by other people, and turned and headed off into the crowd.

Scarlet's pocket vibrated, and she pulled out her cell. As she saw the number, her heart stopped.

It was her dad.

It took her breath away. She didn't know what to do. There was no way he'd be calling her, unless he knew. Somehow, he must have got into her room and saw she wasn't there.

Oh no, she thought. *He must be freaking out.*

"What's wrong?" Maria asked; she must've seen her expression.

"My parents," she said.

Maria shrugged. "Whatever," she said. "It's not even that late."

But Scarlet was not so nonchalant; she wondered how she'd cover up the smell of alcohol on her breath, or cigarette on her clothes. She wondered if she should answer the phone or ignore it. Neither was a good option. She decided to ignore it. Better to try to explain later, in person.

"OMG, there's Blake!" Maria yelled, grabbing Scarlet by the shoulder and pointing to the far corner of another room.

Scarlet's heart started to pound as she spotted him, standing with his buddies by the keg, getting a refill. Luckily, he hadn't seen her yet. Now that she saw him, here in the flesh, she wasn't sure if she wanted him to. She was having second thoughts. After what happened, she wasn't even sure how she felt about him. She had apologized and he had ignored it. That was rude. He hadn't answered her texts and he'd been acting like she didn't existed. For her, that was too much. It made her really think twice about whether she liked him at all.

And ever since meeting Sage, it became a lot easier to forget about Blake.

"What are you waiting for?" Maria prodded. "Go up to him. Vivian's not here. This is your chance."

"I don't really feel like it," Scarlet replied.

"What are you talking about? Tomorrow's the big dance. He'd standing right there. What are you waiting for?"

Scarlet was starting to resent all the pressure.

"You're hardly one to talk," she finally snapped. "It's not like you asked Sage out."

Maria frowned.

"I'm done chasing him," Scarlet said. "If he wants to approach me, he will. If he doesn't, that's fine."

"So then what, are you like not even gonna go to the dance?" Maria asked.

"Would that be the end of the world?" Scarlet replied.

Maria shrugged.

"I'm gonna look for Sage. I'll be back. Will you be here?"

"I think I might wander a bit," Scarlet said. "Maybe get some air."

"Okay, I'll do a quick tour of duty, then find you."

Scarlet wandered out of the kitchen, into the adjoining sitting room, the music getting louder. She weaved between the bodies and made her way out to the back deck. She set down her barely-drank wine cooler in a dark corner. She really didn't want to drink tonight, or get into the habit. She didn't need it. She could enjoy herself without it.

It was good to be out here, in the fresh air, especially since inside was so hot and steamy. A small group of kids congregated back here, but they were engrossed in their own conversation and kept to themselves.

Leaning on the railing, she looked out across the backyard. She watched the large oak trees swaying in the wind, and behind them, caught glimpses of the full moon. It was a beautiful night.

"There you are," came the voice.

Scarlet's heart pounded as she recognized the voice. Blake.

She slowly turned and saw him standing there, dressed in jeans and a hoodie, a shark-tooth necklace at the base of his throat. He held a cup of beer in one hand, and Scarlet could tell from his expression that he'd already had a few.

"I heard you were here," he said. "Why didn't you say hi?"

Scarlet stared back at him, wondering if she'd heard correctly. Was he kidding? Was he playing mind games?

"Why should I?" she said, proud of herself for standing up to him.

He took a step closer, a little off-balance, and looked at her. As she looked into his blue eyes, she momentarily felt her old feelings for him; but she forced herself to look away.

"You're the one that took off," he said. "I figured you weren't into me."

She thought about how to respond. Finally, she had a chance to explain.

"I'm sorry," she said. "I really am. I didn't mean to hurt you. I was actually having a really good time. It was just…"

Scarlet hesitated, wondering how to phrase it.

"Just what?" he said. "I'm not good enough for you?"

"No, it's nothing like that," she said. "It was just…I got really sick. I can't explain it. I just didn't feel well."

He looked at her, and for the first time, his expression softened.

"Why didn't you just say so?" he asked.

"I tried," she snapped, her anger rising, "but you never replied to my text."

He looked down, as if with regret. "You're right. If I knew…." He trailed off.

"Anyway, you didn't have to go saying those things about me, to Vivian," Scarlet said. "That you dumped me and all that."

His eyes opened wide. "I never said that."

"It was all over Facebook."

He shrugged. "She made it up. It wasn't me. I can't control her."

"Then why didn't you go online and say something?" Scarlet asked, relieved he hadn't said it, but still mad.

He looked down, guilty.

"Listen," he said, "let's just forget all that. The past is the past. I came out here because I wanted to talk to you. About the dance tomorrow night. I was—"

"So, *this* is where you're hiding," suddenly came a voice.

Oh no, Scarlet thought. *Not her. Not now.*

She turned and saw, standing there, her worst nightmare: Vivian. Flanked by two of her friends. Her eyes were bloodshot, and she was clearly drunk. The three of them marched out onto the back deck, as she strutted right up to Blake.

"Vivian," he began, "I don't—"

"You don't *what?*" she snapped back, not letting him finish.

"It's just not…" he began, "…it's just not working out."

"What are you talking about?" she spat, fuming. Then she turned and looked at Scarlet, daggers in her eyes. "Are you telling him lies about me?"

Scarlet was taken aback. Here was Vivian, who told lies about everyone else, accusing Scarlet of telling lies about her.

"We weren't talking about you at all," Blake said, in her defense.

Finally, Scarlet thought. Blake was *finally* standing up for her.

"Don't lie," Vivian snapped, turning back to Blake. "Remember what you said to me the other day. I don't think you want me repeating it," she threatened, staring right at Blake.

Blake's face turned red and Scarlet wondered it was he'd said.

"Anyway, this is between me and her," Vivian snapped, looking back at Scarlet. "Go get me a drink," she ordered Blake.

Blake stood there, debating. Scarlet could see that this was his moment. This was his time to stand up to her for good, to be the man that Scarlet needed him to be.

But his eyes glazed over in defeat, and she could see in that moment that he just didn't have the courage to stand up to Vivian. There was just something about her that overpowered him.

Blake slinked away, back into the house, leaving Scarlet alone to face Vivian and her friends. It was an act that Scarlet would never forgive him for.

Scarlet's face flushed red. Not only was she furious at Vivian, but she was supremely disappointed in Blake. That certainly wasn't the quality she wanted in a boyfriend. And for the first time, she wondered if she was wrong to have any feelings for Blake at all. For the first time, she wondered, if he asked her to the dance, if she would even say yes.

"If you think you can waltz in here and steal Blake away from me, you're mistaken," Vivian said, inching closer to Scarlet, slurring her words. "You're a loser. A nobody. You wouldn't even have been invited here if your friend wasn't dating Jake. Good luck going to the dance tomorrow night without a date."

Vivian leaned in closer, so close that Scarlet could smell the vodka on her breath.

"And if you get in my way with Blake again, that little posting online will be nothing compared to what's going to come. Every single day, for the rest of the year," she hissed at Scarlet, with utter venom.

Scarlet stood there, fuming, wondering how to respond. She was too furious to even know what to say. A part of her wanted to punch Vivian and all of her disgusting friends. But of course, she wouldn't do that. She was classier than that. She had to fight fire with fire, to use her words.

"Well, if you're going to post again, why don't you try the truth: that Blake's not into you, that you made up all those things about me—and that you're a miserable person."

"You little witch," she hissed, taking a step forward.

Scarlet prepared to defend herself. She could feel a sudden power surging through her veins, and sensed that she could really hurt Vivian if she wanted to. But she didn't want to. She just wanted her to disappear.

Suddenly the sliding glass door opened, and out strutted Maria.

"Well oh well, look who it is," Maria said to Vivian. "If it isn't the wicked witch herself!"

Vivian and her friends turned and looked as Maria walked out.

"Well, if it isn't the second loser of the pair," Vivian snapped back.

Maria didn't hesitate. She hoisted her plastic cup, filled with beer, and to Scarlet's surprise, threw it right in Vivian's face.

Vivian screamed, her face and hair and clothes soaked.

Everyone on the deck, a good dozen people, turned and watched, stunned into silence.

Then they burst out into laughter, laughing in Vivian's face.

Vivian suddenly shrieked and leapt for Maria, raising her claws high and aiming them right for her face. Vivian was a big girl, nearly six feet tall, and Maria was short and petite, and Scarlet sensed that it would be a disaster.

Scarlet burst into action. Without even realizing what she was doing, she reacted lightning fast. As Vivian brought her hand down for Maria's face, Scarlet caught it at the last second.

Scarlet held Vivian's wrist with her super-strength, preventing her hand from reaching Maria.

And then, she pushed Vivian back.

It wasn't a hard push, but it nonetheless sent her flying back, into her two friends. The three of them fell, like dominoes, falling on top of each other on the deck.

Scarlet stood over them, seething with rage, wanting to finish them off.

But she didn't. As the three of them sat up, looking at her, wide-eyed, everyone else on the deck stared at Scarlet, too, as if she were some kind of freak.

"OMG, Scarlet, how did you do that?" Maria asked, with a trembling voice.

But Scarlet had enough. This party was going from bad to worse, and she felt out of control. She stormed into the house, weaved her way through all the pulsating bodies, out the front door, and across the front lawn. She had to get away. Not to mention her phone wouldn't stop vibrating in her pocket, and her parents wouldn't leave her alone. She realized it was time to go, and face the fire.

Suddenly, a voice stopped her from behind.

"Hey," said the voice.

Scarlet stopped in her tracks.

No. It can't be. Not him. Not now.

She turned slowly, hoping it would be anybody but him.

Her heart was pounding in her throat as she saw him standing there.

Sage.

Dressed in his leather jacket, jeans and leather boots, Sage's longish hair framed his gray eyes, which sparkled down at her.

"Where were you going?" he asked.

"I don't know," she replied, caught off guard, not thinking clearly.

"Surely you must have been going somewhere," he said, and broke into a smile. It was the most beautiful smile she had ever seen.

It was contagious; she found herself smiling back.

"I guess, anywhere but here. I've had my drama for the day."

"I know what you mean. I'm not really one for parties myself."

"So why are you here?" she asked, surprised.

"I was hoping to find someone," he said.

She stared back, mesmerized, wondering.

"Who?" she asked.

He paused, then, in his soft voice, he said, "You, actually."

Me? Scarlet thought. *Why?*

Her throat went dry.

So. He felt the same way.

Scarlet started to worry what would happen if Maria came out and saw the two of them talking. It would be a disaster. She felt she had to get out of here. But she couldn't pull herself away.

"I wanted to talk today," he said. "After class. But you never gave me a chance."

Scarlet didn't know how to respond. She could hardly believe this was happening.

"I'm sorry," she said, knowing how he felt. "I really didn't mean to be rude. It's just that…well…my friend, Maria. She really likes you."

There. She said it. Now he had his chance to go after Maria, if he wanted to.

"But you're the one that I like," he said, staring into her eyes.

As he said it, he took a step closer, reached up with his palm and caressed her cheek. Scarlet's heart was pounding in her throat. She felt frozen in time.

"Scarlet?" came an outraged voice.

She turned, and her heart dropped to see Maria standing there, just a few feet away, staring with a mix of confusion and outrage. Maria looked utterly horrified, as if Scarlet had just stabbed her in the back. Scarlet could see in her eyes how deeply betrayed she felt.

Scarlet immediately felt guilty, even though she knew she hadn't done anything wrong.

"Maria, you don't understand—" Scarlet began.

But it was too late. Maria burst into tears and stormed off. She disappeared back into the crowd.

Scarlet felt a pit in her stomach. She knew Maria, and knew she would never forgive something like this. She would perceive it as a betrayal, and would never get over it. Scarlet felt wracked by guilt and sadness, as she had a sinking feeling that Maria would never talk to her again—and would also turn all her friends against her. She felt more alone than ever.

"You okay?" Sage asked.

Scarlet wiped a tear, and turned and looked back at Sage, who was still staring at her with his haunting, gray eyes. She nodded, trying to snap out of it and back into the moment. But it wasn't working.

"I have to get home," she said. "I'm sorry."

"Home can wait," he said. "Come with me."

He held out a hand.

Scarlet was stunned. She looked down at his open hand. Her relationship with Maria was already ruined, and clearly, nothing would fix that. At the same time, her feelings for Blake were almost nonexistent. Sage was the one who mesmerized her. He was the one who cared. He was the one she wanted to be with.

Her cell buzzed again and again in her pocket. She knew she should go back home, forget about this night, patch things up with her parents, try to patch things up with Maria. Try to force life back to normal.

But she was tired of normal. She was so tired of trying to control everyone and everything, trying to make life run so perfectly. She'd had enough. She felt like letting go now. Letting the universe take her wherever it wanted to.

So, to her own surprise, she reached out her cold hand and placed it gently in his palm.

She had no idea where he would take her, but she had a feeling it would be different than any place she had ever been. As she looked down at his open palm, she knew, she just knew, that this would be the night that changed everything.

CHAPTER NINE

Caitlin sat there in her living room, in a daze, feeling the world spinning out of control beneath her. More and more, she felt as if she were living in a dream, far removed from reality, trying to grasp hold of the events happening around her. Some days, she felt as if she were losing her mind.

That episode in the church was real. It was very, very real. Those blown-out candles, those shattered windows, were the first tangible thing she could point to to prove to herself that she was not crazy. That her daughter was a vampire. Even the priest had fled. For once, her fears had been confirmed by someone else.

That was all she needed. Now, finally, she felt confident in herself, felt certain about what was happening to Scarlet. Regardless of what Caleb, or anyone else thought, she was more determined than ever to save her daughter before it was too late.

Caleb paced their living room in a manic state, talking to one person after the next on his cell. She had never seen him so worried. When Scarlet hadn't answered her door, he'd actually put his shoulder into it, breaking it open, terrified that she was sick, or needed help. But when he'd found her room empty, her window open, and realized she'd lied and snuck out—he'd lost it. He went from worried to furious. Now he was on a mission to find her.

Caitlin was worried, too—but this time she wasn't perplexed. Now, she understood. She knew what was happening to Scarlet. She was changing. Turning. This behavior, in some ways, was to be expected. She wasn't worried for Scarlet's safety out there—she was worried for the safety of others, of whomever might cross her path.

While Caleb paced the house, calling everyone he knew, Caitlin took a different approach. She knew that what mattered, in the big picture, wasn't finding Scarlet right now. She knew Scarlet would eventually come back, on her own terms. She knew that what really mattered was finding out how to cure Scarlet—if there even was a cure. She thought again of the torn page from that rare book, and again debated whether the other half existed—and whether it would really even help.

Caitlin opened her folder and pulled out the page, dissecting it again. She ran her hand along the edges of the frail paper, feeling its thick, rough edges, yellowed with age. She felt along the tear mark, wracking her brain, willing herself to come up with any clues, any leads. But she kept drawing a blank.

As her mind spun, trying to think again of anyone who might be of help, inevitably she focused on one person: Aiden. He was the only one in the world who would know what the page meant, whether the other half existed, and where to look for it. Knowing him, he was probably already familiar with this book—and could probably tell her more about it than she could discover with months of research.

She trembled at the thought of calling him. They had left on such bad terms, she was embarrassed, afraid, to talk to him. A part of her was still mad at him; another part felt he was the only one left who could help her.

She checked her watch: 11 PM. He was probably asleep. She wondered if he would even take her call if he was awake.

But the more she pondered it, the more she felt an urgency to talk to him. She had to swallow her pride. She had to know where this page was. She only hoped that he wouldn't corner her in with more talk of stopping Scarlet. If he did, she would hang up on him, and never speak to him again. But she had to give him one more chance.

Her heart pounded in her throat as she took out her cell and tapped on his name.

She held the phone to her ear as it rang. She waited, her heart pounding, a part of her hoping he wouldn't answer.

Finally, there came a sound of the other end, a fumbling of the phone. After a long pause, a groggy voice said: "Caitlin. I was wondering when you would call."

"I'm sorry," she said. "For storming out like that. You were just trying to help me. I realize that. But when you talked about stopping Scarlet…well… I couldn't hear it. I still can't. I won't entertain the idea of stopping her. Never. I'd rather kill myself first."

There was a long silence on the other end.

"I think I've found another way," she added.

"Tell me."

"Have you heard of Vairo's *De Fascino Libri Tres*?" she asked, hoping, praying, that he had.

"Of course," came his immediate, confident reply, to her great relief. "It was published in the late sixteenth century. Vairo was a bishop. But what most people don't know is that he had also studied mathematics and philosophy and science from the time he was a child. He, in turn, was influenced by Plato and Socrates and, to some extent, Hippocrates—and there is some evidence his theories influence Isaac Newton a century later. *De Fascino* was considered the seminal work of its time. You very rarely get a hold of it these days. Why do you ask?"

Caitlin felt so relieved; she had made the right move to call him.

"I have a copy here, in our school library," she said.

He paused, and she could sense he was impressed.

"I stumbled across something in it. It's like a ritual, a ceremony. He claims it will heal the afflicted from vampirism. But the thing is, the page with the ceremony is torn in half. And the other half is missing. It's an original edition—our library has it on loan—and our database shows no other existing copy. I need to see the other half of that page."

She paused, and a long silence followed. She hoped he'd have a solution. She knew that if anyone would, it would be him. He was her best and last hope.

The silence went on so long, for a moment, she wondered if he'd hung up. Just as she was about to ask, his voice rang out:

"There are two issues here. The first is whether this so-called ritual has any merit. Despite his insistence on impartiality, in truth, Vairo's was a highly biased, very controversial work. We have no proof that anything in it was accurate. Keep in mind, too, that some of it was borrowed, some passed down, and some may have even been plagiarized. The chances of such a ritual working are remote. Of course, there's always hope. I would not say it's impossible. But I think the likelihood is negligible."

"But there's hope?" she asked. "You admit that there's at least a slim possibility?"

"Yes," he answered. "Certainly, there are some rituals and formulas in that book which scholars have been unable to discount, despite centuries of trying. So, yes. While remote, there is hope.

"But you still have the second issue, which is finding the other edition. You are overlooking one very important fact, of course: what most people don't realize is that Vairo's work was, in fact, published in two editions. I assume your edition is Venice, 1589?"

Caitlin paused, taken aback.

"Yes, it is."

"What most people don't realize is that that was, in fact, the second edition. The first edition is much more rare. It was published in Paris, in 1583. Thus, a second edition does indeed exist."

Caitlin was speechless, blown away by his scholarship, as she always was. She had no idea there was an earlier version.

"But why is there no mention of that anywhere?" she asked.

"It's an unofficial copy," he said.

Caitlin tried to understand. "Unofficial?"

"There are a few volumes in the world so important that their existence is not public knowledge. These are passed down through generations, held by a network of rare occult bookkeepers. These are volumes they don't want the public to get a hold of, volumes they would never admit they had. I doubt any library or university would have one. And I doubt any rare bookshop would have any edition officially on record. But that doesn't mean they don't have it. You would just need to come to them with the right credentials."

"So are you saying that the other copy definitely exists?" she asked, her heart beating.

"I'm not saying there is—I'm saying there is a chance. And if anyone has it, it would be Rose. She runs the rare bookshop in Marais, on 6 Rue Charlemagne."

Caitlin's eyes opened wide surprise.

"Paris?" she asked

"Yes. It's their oldest rare bookshop, with the most esoteric occult volumes in the world. She would never admit this to a stranger, but she has a back room. For volumes she doesn't make public. If you ask her, she'll deny it. But if you use my name, and express the urgency of your mission, she just might let you in. It's your best bet."

"But Paris?" she asked, overwhelmed at the thought. "Before I go all the way there, maybe I can just call her and she'd tell me if she even hasn't it. And then maybe fax it to me? Or scan it?"

Aiden sighed.

"She must be nearly a hundred years old by now, and she doesn't use technology. In fact, you're lucky if she even answers the door. Most of the time, her storefront is gated. But that doesn't mean she's not there. She only opens for certain people. She won't fax or scan anything. She won't even answer her phone. I'm sorry, but there's no other way. You'd have to go."

"Thank you, Aiden," she said, meaningfully. "Really."

"I hope it works," he said. "I truly do."

He hung up, and she sat there, her mind racing. Clearly, there was no other choice: she had to go to Paris.

Caleb entered, putting his phone down.

"What are you doing?" he snapped at her. She didn't like the tone of his voice. "I'm calling frantically for Scarlet, and you're just sitting here. Don't you care about our daughter?"

Caitlin stood, ready to pack her things. "I care more than you'll ever know."

"I'm calling and calling her, and she's not picking up," Caleb said, pacing again. "I've called all her friends and their parents and nobody knows a thing. I just got off the phone with Samantha, who checked her Facebook for me. Apparently, there's a lot of chatter about a house party tonight. At the Wilsons. I think she's there. I think she's with that boy, Blake—I think he's the source of all this trouble."

"That's ridiculous," Caitlin said. "Blake has nothing to do with this."

She crossed the room, gathering books and papers into her briefcase.

"Well I'm going over there," Caleb said. "I'm going to find her and bring her back."

He stopped and looked up at her.

"Where are you going?" he asked, looking at her briefcase, incredulous. "To work?"

"To Paris," she replied.

"*Paris?*" he asked, dumbfounded. "Are you joking?"

"No," she answered, busy packing, not having time for his questions and not caring what he thought. She knew he'd just try to stop her. "There's a book I need there. I think it can help Scarlet."

"A book? In Paris? Have you lost your mind?"

He stared at her as if she had three heads.

"Listen," Caitlin said, trying to explain, "you don't know what happened at church today. When Scarlet was there, the windows— they shattered. Our daughter did that. Don't you realize? After all this time? That none of this is a coincidence? Scarlet is becoming a vampire. And I'm the only one who can save her."

"You're sick," Caleb stammered. "You need help. You really do. You're falling apart. I can't believe it, at a time like this, when we need you the most. You're just going to abandon ship, with our daughter lost out there, and fly to Paris?" he asked, his voice rising.

"You still don't understand," she shot back, her own voice rising: "My going to Paris is the only thing that will save her."

Caleb stood there, looking crushed.

"I don't even know who you are anymore."

His words stung Caitlin, and she felt like crying. She felt their relationship was breaking apart.

She couldn't stand another minute of this. So without another word, she snatched her briefcase, strutted out the door and hurried to her car, intent on catching the next flight to Paris.

CHAPTER TEN

Scarlet's heart beat with excitement as they pulled up to Sage's mansion. He had driven her here from the party, and she recalled the shocking moment when she'd first seen his car: a black Lamborghini. She'd never seen one before. As she had sat in it, sinking into the hard, leather seats, so low to the ground, she couldn't help feeling as if her life were becoming more and more surreal.

She had never met anyone who had owned a car like this—and in fact, had never met a boy who seemed as mature and ageless—and mysterious—as Sage. Everything he did just made him more mysterious. Every question she had just led to more questions. How could it be that he was driving a Lamborghini? Was he that wealthy?

They had barely spoken during the drive, which only deepened the sense of mystery.

He'd driven her down familiar village streets, then made a few unfamiliar terms, taking her down roads she rarely drove on in all her time growing up here. The roads twisted and turned and before she knew it they were on the famous river road, on which sat the largest and most expensive mansions overlooking the Hudson River. After a few more miles, he turned off into one of them.

Now, the huge wrought iron gate was slowly opening before them.

She could hardly take it all in. She'd never been to any of these mansions in her entire life, and hadn't known anyone who'd lived in them. Now here was this boy, Sage, appearing out of nowhere, in his black Lamborghini, and taking her to one of the biggest and grandest of them all.

As they drove down the driveway, it seemed like it took forever. His front lawn was the size of a state park, and they passed under rows of mature trees, sheltering the driveway. The moonlight peaked through the branches as they went, and finally, the house came into view.

It was not a house: it was a sprawling stone mansion, stretching out in multiple wings. Behind it, its huge lawn sloped down to the Hudson River. It was the most beautiful home she'd ever seen; it looked like it belonged in a fairytale.

She could not believe that Sage lived here. And she could not believe that he had picked her, of all the girls. It almost felt too good to be true. She had a million questions she was burning to ask him, but didn't even know where to begin.

"Is this like your parents' house?" she asked.

"Some of the time," he responded cryptically.

Just like him: every question just led to more questions.

"What does that mean?" she pressed.

She didn't want to be nosy, but at the same time she felt that if she were going to get close to him, she needed some straight answers. She needed to know who she was with.

"We have houses around the world. We don't stay in this one that often anymore."

He had given her an answer, but of course, it just led to more questions. She figured she'd stop for now; she didn't want it to seem as if she were interrogating him.

He pulled up in front of the house and they got out and walked towards it. There was a soft glow coming from inside.

"Are your parents home?" she asked, puzzled.

"They're out for the night. My entire…family went out tonight."

"Do you have brothers and sisters?" she asked.

"One sister. And lots of cousins."

"Do they all live here?" she asked, wondering how such a small family could live in such a huge house.

"Sometimes," he replied. "They come and go a lot. It's hard to keep track."

Again, his answer just made her want to know more; but she held back for now.

He grabbed the ornate brass knocker and yanked open the arched oak door, at least a foot thick. It creaked, and she felt as if he were opening a door to another world.

They stepped inside and he closed the door behind them, slamming it shut with a bang.

They entered a cavernous, stone parlor, lit by a low-hanging, candle chandelier, all the candles flickering. She looked left and right, and saw that the series of open rooms stretched forever, candle sconces all along the stone walls flickering, giving the rooms a soft, warm glow. There was no other lighting, and the rooms were dim. She also spotted huge, marble mantle fireplaces on either end of the room, each with a glow of a dying fire.

It was the most beautiful house she had ever been in. She hardly knew what to make of it: the rooms were pieces of dark, antique furniture; there was a four-poster bed in the middle of the living room, a chaise lounge on the far wall before the fireplace, huge, ornate mirrors and Persian rugs covering sections of stone. She felt as if she'd entered a Medieval museum.

She looked over at Sage and wondered about him. Did he really live here? What was this place?

In the far corner, she spotted a black, Steinway piano. From its thick legs it looked to be several hundred years old. She was suddenly curious.

"Do you play?" she asked. She'd always wanted to learn to play. She'd started listening to classical music lately, between her pop, and found it relaxing, especially before bedtime.

He shrugged. "A little."

"Can you play something?" she asked. "I'd like to hear it."

He hesitated.

"Come on," she goaded.

He walked slowly over to the piano and looked at it longingly, as if he hadn't touched it in years. After a long pause, he finally sat at the bench.

Sage wiped a thick layer of dust off the lid, then slowly opened it and pushed it back. He looked down at the keys, closed his eyes and breathed deeply. It was as if memories were coming back to him.

"I'll play you something from my childhood," he said.

Scarlet came over and stood beside him. As she stood there, she looked out through the floor-to-ceiling windows at the moon, illuminating him at the piano. Through the old, warped glass she saw the huge backyard, framed by oak trees, sloping down towards the river—and beyond it, the glistening Hudson.

Sage began to play, and the music took her breath away. She was transported. It was the most beautiful melody she'd ever heard, slow and soft and dark, and the more he played, the more relaxed she felt. As the notes filled the air, all the stress of the last few days began to pour out of her. All the tension with her parents, the stress of her being sick, her fighting with Vivian, with Maria…it all slowly left.

When he finished, a peaceful silence filled the room. The grandfather clock ticked several seconds before she could open her eyes again.

"That was beautiful," she said.

He smiled, then quickly closed the lid, as if embarrassed.

"It's been a long time," he said.

"What song was that?"

"Beethoven," he said. "The Moonlight Sonata. You should have heard him play it," he added nostalgically, looking off into the distance as if remembering.

Scarlet was confused.

"Um…hasn't he been dead a long time?" she asked. "How could you have heard him play it?"

He seemed caught off guard.

"I meant…um…what I meant to say was that I heard a recording of him playing it."

But Sage looked flustered, as if caught in a lie. And as Scarlet thought about it, it seemed odd—they didn't have recording devices hundreds of years ago. How could he have heard Beethoven playing it?

But he quickly got up from the piano and took her hand, and began to lead her through the house—and her focus changed. The feel of his hand on hers was electrifying: it was hard to think of anything else.

She was nervous as he led her through all the rooms, and wondered where he was taking her. Could he be leading her to her bedroom? If so, what would she say?

Scarlet got even more nervous as she started to think about how attracted she felt to him. She thought back to her time with Blake, by the river, of how she had changed. Wanted his blood. She felt so nervous that something like that might happen again—this time with Sage. She couldn't allow that to happen. She couldn't ruin things. Not twice. She willed her body to stay normal. She prayed that she wouldn't suddenly freak out again and have to run out of here.

Please God. Make me be normal. Just tonight. Just let me get through this.

Finally, Sage led her to a set of tall, French doors. He reached up, unlocked the antique brass hardware, slid the bolts and turned the delicate knobs. He pulled open both doors and took her hand and led her outside onto the wide, stone terrace.

The night air was crisp and refreshing. The terrace stretched forever, fifty feet in each direction, and culminated in a wide, marble railing.

He led her to it and as they leaned against it, she looked out at the huge full moon over the Hudson, the water sparkling. The air was filled with the sound of the ancient trees swaying in the wind.

Scarlet felt as if she'd walked into a postcard. She wanted to freeze this moment forever.

It also made her feel a more pressing need for answers. Who was this boy, really? Was this all too good to be true?

"Tell me about you," Scarlet said, as she turned and faced him. His mysterious grey eyes were glistening, reflecting the color of the moon as he looked out at the horizon.

"Like what?" he asked.

"Anything. Everything. I really don't know anything. You're so...mysterious. Nobody really knows anything. It's like you just showed up one day, out of nowhere. Tell me about you. Your past. Where you're from. Your family. It's all so...different. You're so different from everyone around here. Don't you see that?"

He looked away, and she hoped she hadn't pushed too far. But she was dying to know, and she had to ask.

"I don't understand why different isn't okay," he answered.

"It's fine, I don't care. I guess I just want to know who I'm with."

He sighed.

"My family is pretty intense. I'm sorry. I wish I could tell you more but I can't. Maybe one day I'll be able to, and you'll understand."

Scarlet was beginning to feel disappointed. She *didn't* understand. Why couldn't he tell her?

"What I can tell you is this," he continued, "I know it's hard to believe, because we barely know each other, but I care about you. Very much."

He turned and looked into her eyes, and the full force of his stare was overwhelming. She felt butterflies.

"The first second I saw you, in the cafeteria, and when I saw you again outside your house, I felt like I knew you. Like we're connected somehow."

He looked into her eyes and as he did, Scarlet felt her heart pounding. It was eerie, because that was the exact same thing she had been thinking. And she didn't understand how it was possible, either. It made no sense. They barely knew each other. How could they have such strong feelings?

"Do you feel it, too?" he asked.

Scarlet hesitated, not knowing how to respond. She got nervous.

"Maybe," she said, her voice trembling.

He reached up with one hand and gently brushed the hair from her face. As he did, he ran his fingertips along her cheek—and his touch was electrifying. She could barely breathe as he took a step closer, leaned in. He came closer and closer, and she leaned in, too, just a bit.

And for the first time, their lips met.

Their kiss sent an electric shock throughout her entire body, and she felt everything she knew about the world starting to change. First, it was a soft, gentle kiss, then he kissed harder, and so did she. She closed her eyes, and felt her world melting.

She feared she might transform again, might be overwhelmed with a desire to feed on him, as she had been with Blake.

But to her relief and surprise, the desire never came. She couldn't understand why, and she was beyond grateful. Her prayer had been answered. She was normal again.

Suddenly, to her surprise, Sage backed away. He suddenly took two steps back, turned from her, and faced the river. As he did, he raised one hand to his chest, and looked to be in pain.

She was confused. Had she done something wrong? Was he sick?

"What's wrong?" she asked.

She came over and placed a hand on his back, wondering if he was okay. She was shocked: as fate would have it, the roles had reversed. He was the one that was suddenly backing away—not her.

"I'm sorry," he said.

"What is it?" she asked, wondering if it was her. Had he changed his mind?

"I wish I could tell you," he said. "I'm sorry," he added. "But I have to go."

Scarlet stared back, shocked.

"Did I do something wrong?" she asked.

He shook his head.

"It's not you," he answered. "It's my…family."

"Your family?" she asked, confused.

He closed his eyes, as if in pain, and slowly shook his head again.

"I'm sorry. Here. Please. Take my car. Bring yourself home. You have to leave now. I'm sorry."

She looked at him as he held out the keys to his Lamborghini, flabbergasted and hurt.

"I can't take your car," she said, shocked. "I don't even have my driver's license. And it's like a million dollar car."

"It's okay. Take it and bring it back tomorrow. You have to go now. I'm sorry. Please. Go."

He held out the keys to her, and would not even look in her direction.

Scarlet's heart was breaking. She had never felt more confused.

She reached up and took the keys, her hand shaking.

She slowly walked across the patio, heading back towards the house. Her heart was breaking, and at the same time she felt rejected, crushed. And more perplexed than anything.

If anyone should understand suddenly feeling sick, suddenly running away, it should be her. But she didn't. She didn't understand it at all. And she already felt tears welling up as she realized she might never be with Sage again.

CHAPTER ELEVEN

Caitlin sat on the airplane, waiting for it to take off, and checked her cell yet again. She felt so guilty for leaving Caleb like this, especially with Scarlet missing—and felt especially guilty leaving the country. She couldn't remember the last time she'd gone overseas, especially without Caleb. She couldn't help but feel like a criminal, fleeing in the night. She was starting to have doubts if she was doing the right thing.

Caitlin kept trying to text and call Scarlet, as she had the entire way to the airport. She'd tried texting and calling Caleb, too. Neither answered. Caleb, she assumed, was just mad at her; but Scarlet, she feared, was out of touch. She felt that if there were any good news, she would have heard already. Her heart sank further as she sat there.

She hoped that when she got back, she could patch things up with Caleb. Explain it all to him, that he would believe her this time, understand. And that they could get their marriage and family back on the right track, put this whole nightmare behind them. When it was all over, she vowed to herself, she would burn her vampire journals, and never look at them again.

She reminded herself that she was doing this for Scarlet. She pulled out the torn page from her folder and examined it beneath the bright overhead light. She read it again and again, reading and re-reading the ancient ritual to cure a vampire. It seemed authentic. She prayed that it was. And she prayed that Scarlet, out there somewhere, hadn't turned anyone yet. If she had, this ritual would be useless. She only hoped she could get to Paris, find the other half of the page, and get back in time to rescue her daughter.

"I'm sorry ma'am, but you'll have to turn off all electronic devices," came the voice.

Caitlin looked up and saw the flight attendant looking down at her, waiting. She checked her phone one last time:

No new messages.

Reluctantly, she powered it off, as the attendant left.

As the plane began to taxi, she felt a surge of anxiety. Was she just wasting time? Would this old bookstore in Paris even have the book? If so, would they have the missing page? Would the old woman even let her in? Was this all just a wild goose chase?

And most of all: if she found it, would it work?

Caitlin second-guessed herself even as the plane lifted into the air. She looked at her watch and realized she had nine hours until the plane touched down in Paris.

Those nine hours couldn't come fast enough.

CHAPTER TWELVE

Sage sat there, on the wide stone patio, watching the moon drop against the Hudson. He had hardly moved since Scarlet had left. He couldn't help feeling as if he'd messed it all up—and at the worst possible moment.

His heart was breaking inside. He felt closer to Scarlet than to anyone he'd ever encountered in his time on earth, and it had all been going so well. Looking into her eyes and kissing her had been the highlight of centuries.

And then, at the worst possible time, he had gotten struck with the pain. This last year, this final year of his life, the pains had been getting worse, coming more frequently and getting stronger the closer he came to his death date. Now, with just weeks left to live, the pains had become more intense and unpredictable—not just for him, but for every member of his clan. They came out of nowhere and sometimes, they were crippling.

How could he possibly explain that to Scarlet? What was he supposed to say? Was he supposed to tell her that he was an Immortalist? That he had been alive for nearly two thousand years? That he was struck with pain because he would be dead in just a few weeks? That his family had sent him here, to this place, to try to manipulate her, to gain her trust, to find out her secrets—and then kill her?

Of course, that was something he would never do. The moment he'd laid eyes on her, he knew he could never harm her. On the contrary, he'd felt that she was the love of his life, and only regretted that he'd met her with such little time left to live. Even if it meant his own death, he would go the end of the world to protect her. He would never try to get the necklace. If he did, then his clan would surely kill her. And that he could not allow.

So instead, he'd had to send her away like that, so abruptly, without even having a chance to explain. The thought of it broke his heart.

He sat there, slumped against the stone, head in his hands, and barely moved.

"There you are," came the disapproving voice of his father.

"Figured we'd find you here," echoed his mother.

Sage looked up, too tired, in too much emotional pain, to care. Still, his stomach twisted and turned at the sound of their voices. He could already sense their upset.

"Leave me alone," he said, lowering his head.

A split second later, they managed to cross the entire balcony, and his father yanked him by the arm to his feet.

"You had her here," he hissed, "and didn't even try to obtain the necklace."

"You acted like a stupid schoolboy in love," his mother added.

"We have no time," his dad said. "Don't you realize? She holds the key. And you—you sit here playing your pathetic schoolboy games."

"I'm sorry," he said, trying to buy time, to think of how to deter them. "I was waiting for the right time. Then I get struck with the pains."

"She's the one we've been searching for for two thousand years. She holds the key to life, for all of us. You must get her to give you the necklace. Do you understand me?"

It was his father, placing a firm hand on his shoulder, staring down and talking down to him like he always had, for thousands of years.

"And what if I don't?" Sage snapped back, feeling rebellious. He'd had enough. He was tired of being bossed around by them for these thousand years. "What are you going to do? Kill me?"

"Worse," his mother snapped. "We'll kill that little girl you like so much."

Sage felt his stomach drop at the thought.

"What good will that do you?" he asked. "The necklace must be given voluntarily for it to work. Killing her won't do you any good."

"Well, if she won't give it, then we have nothing to lose, do we?" his mother asked with an evil smile.

Sage examined their expressions and could see they were serious. The thought of their harming Scarlet was like a knife in his heart. He could see they were getting desperate. They were approaching death, too: he could see the color in their cheeks fading, their bones becoming more pronounced. In a few weeks, they'd be dead. They had nothing left to lose. They were different people now than they were centuries ago. And he feared they meant what they said.

He had to think of a way to stall them. Just long enough so that he could rescue Scarlet, get her far away from here.

"I promise, I'll get the necklace," he said. "Just don't harm her. Just give me a chance."

"You have until tomorrow night," his dad snapped. "If you don't have it by then, she's dead. Lore will gladly do the job."

The two of them turned and marched back into the house. Sage walked them go, then turned back to the river, looking out, contemplating what to do next. He had to save her before it was too late.

"Well well well," came the voice.

He turned and saw Lore ambling towards him. He was clapping, in an exaggerated way.

"Nice theater. Mom and dad bought it, didn't they? Can't fool me, though. You're not going to even try for that necklace. I can tell by that lost puppy-dog look."

He sneered as he got closer, slowly circling him, his leather boots clicking on the stone.

"You're pathetic," he added. "Always have been. Romance died in the Middle Ages, in case someone forgot to give you the memo. She's just human meat. Like all of them. Even if she is a vampire, who cares? She's not one of us."

"Stay away from me, Lore," Sage said, feeling his anger well up. He was in no mood for this right now.

"Gladly. I'll stay away from you—far away, when we're all dead. In the meantime, I'm not as stupid as the others. You can bet I'll kill her the second they give me the green light—if for no other reason than to rile you up. Besides, I like doing things like that. In fact, I like it so much, I might not even wait until tomorrow night. After all, what are they going to do? Punish me?"

He broke into laughter.

Sage couldn't take it any longer. The centuries of Lore's mocking and teasing had finally gotten to him: without thinking, he leapt into the air, reached out and strangled him. He carried him through the air, slamming him into the stone railing.

The railing shattered, and the two of them went down, off the edge, plunging dozens of feet below, and landing hard in the grass.

Lore spun around, and choked Sage. Sage kneed him in the gut, then reached around and knocked him off.

The two of them lay there, on their backs, beside each other, looking up at the moonlit sky, catching their breath. Sage wiped blood off the corner of his mouth. It was useless, he knew that: Lore couldn't be killed. Just like him.

"I love you Sage, you know that?" Lore said, breaking into light laughter.

Just like him, Sage thought. In Lore's sick, demented mind, this was love.

"Stay away from her," Sage spat, getting to his feet slowly, limping across the lawn.

As he walked, already Lore's mocking laughter filled the moonlit sky.

CHAPTER THIRTEEN

Caleb stormed out of his house, livid. He could not believe what was happening to his family, how quickly everything seemed to be changing. Caitlin, who'd been a rock in his life for as long as he had known her, was having a breakdown. He had never seen her like this. All she talked about were vampires, supernatural nonsense, and her belief that her own daughter was turning into a vampire. It was ridiculous. He had been hoping that it was only due to stress, to Scarlet's sickness, and that it would all go away and she would return to normal.

But Caitlin seemed to be getting worse. She wouldn't stop obsessing over it, talking constantly of vampires, and then, bringing Scarlet to church. Now she talked about the priest, and something about the windows breaking. It was crazy. She had really lost it.

If that were not enough, now she was getting on a plane for Paris. Caleb had gone from being merely upset over this to truly worried. He didn't know who he was more worried for now—his daughter or his wife. She had texted him from the plane, but he'd been too mad to respond.

Not to mention Scarlet: he could not understand what had come over her, either. Just a few days ago, she had been the sweet, kind, caring teenage daughter he had always known. He had never known her to act out like this. Slamming doors, yelling at them, skipping school, staying out late. And now, lying to them and sneaking out. This just wasn't her.

He thought back to her being sick, a few days ago, and wondered if somehow it was all related. He thought it was silly to attribute all of this to some mysterious illness. This was no illness. To him, it seemed like drugs. Maybe Scarlet had been experimenting with drugs, like the police said, and maybe that was what had made her sick. Maybe it was some kind of bad trip. That would certainly explain for all her erratic behavior as of late. And the mood swings.

As Caleb walked to his car, and thought about the possibility of her doing drugs, he thought about any new friends that might have come into her life lately. His mind kept returning to one person: Blake. He didn't know of any other new friends, and Blake was the first boyfriend she'd introduced them to. In Caleb's mind, it was too much of a coincidence: one day, she introduces a new boyfriend, and the next, she's acting like a completely different person. He felt certain, deep in his bones, that it was Blake's doing, that he was a drug-addict and a terrible influence. They were probably spending all their time together, and he was probably enticing her to do drugs.

The thought sent him into a rage. He felt certain Scarlet was with Blake, and was determined to track them down and bring her back, and to keep him far away from his daughter.

Caleb floored it, screeching out of the driveway and speeding the ten or so blocks to the Wilsons' house.

As he turned the corner in their quiet, sleepy village, he saw the street lit up: dozens of cars were parked in front, and every light in the house was on. Music blared even from here, and dozens of kids streamed onto the lawn, many holding plastic beer cups.

His rage increased, as he felt certain his daughter was inside. Probably with Blake.

He pulled up and parked in front of the house, jumped out and strutted across the street. He marched up the walkway, to the surprised stares of many teenagers, and scanned the lawn, looking for any sign of Scarlet, or Blake.

Caleb marched up to a girl he recognized as one of Scarlet's friends. She saw him marching up, and she looked surprised—and scared.

"Hello Mr. Paine," she said, lowering her beer cup. "What are you doing here?"

"Is Scarlet here?" he asked abruptly.

"Um…I saw her earlier. I think she's inside," she said, tentatively. "Is everything okay?"

So, Scarlet was here. Caleb was right.

He turned and stormed into the house, marching through the open front door.

The living room was absolutely packed, jammed shoulder to shoulder with kids. He could already see all the damage they'd done in the house, and could only imagine the expressions of the Wilsons when they returned from their trip. He knew them both well—they'd had dinner many times, and knew they'd be devastated to come home to a house like this. Caleb thought it was a shame that their son had done such a thing. *What was it with teenagers?* he wondered.

He pushed his way through the crowd, scanning the faces, looking for any sign of his daughter, or of Blake.

Finally, halfway through the room, he spotted Blake, standing there, in the corner, with a tall blonde girl who seemed to be coming on to him. At least Blake, to his credit, didn't seem interested in her.

The sight of him put Caleb in a rage. He marched right up to him, the crowd parting ways. Blake did a double-take as he saw Caleb, and his expression morphed to one of true fear.

"Mr. Paine," he said.

Caleb marched right up to him, grabbed his shirt with both of his hands, and pulled him in close.

"Where's my daughter?" he growled.

Blake swallowed.

"I don't know. I swear. Why? Is she okay?"

"Don't you lie to me," Caleb said.

"Mr. Paine, I swear. I have no idea. I like Scarlet. I would never do anything—"

"Is that why you invited her here? To get her drunk? To get her high?"

"Whoa dude," Blake said, "it's not like that at all. You've got it wrong. I didn't invite her here. She showed up on her own. Like, look around: the whole school's here."

"You think she would have come if it weren't for you?" Caleb pressed.

Blake's eyes fell in disappointment.

"I like your daughter. I really do. But she's not even into me."

Caleb could see by Blake's expression that he was telling the truth.

Slowly, he relaxed his grip. He still stood there though, glowering down at Blake.

"Have you offered my daughter any drugs, at any time in the last several days?" he asked.

"No sir. I would never do that."

"Except for that hit on the joint you handed her the other day," came a girl's snotty voice.

Caleb turned and saw that blonde girl standing there, looking drunk, a sneer on her face.

"Hate to be the one to say it," she added. "But it's true."

Caleb turned and glowered back at Blake. He could tell by his guilty expression that it was true.

"It wasn't like that," Blake said. "There was like a big group of us. Someone was passing around a joint. It wasn't me."

Caleb's face turned red, as he felt himself fill with fury and rage. He had caught him in a lie. He was a drug addict. He had been pushing drugs on his daughter. Caleb had been right all along. If this boy was any older, Caleb would beat him to a pulp. It took every ounce of his will to contain himself.

"I'm only going to say this once," Caleb sneered. "Stay away from my daughter. Do you hear me? I find you anywhere near here, and you're dead. You understand?"

Slowly, Blake nodded, looking ashen.

Caleb turned and stormed back through the house, shoving his way through the party. He looked everywhere, but saw no signs of Scarlet. It looked like she'd left. But with who?

Caleb stormed out the house, down the walkway, and was trying to figure out where to go next, when suddenly there came a voice.

"OMG, Mr. Paine?"

Caleb turned, recognizing it. It was Maria. Scarlet's best friend.

"Like what are you doing here?" she added

"Maria," he said with urgency, heading towards her. "It's important. I need to know where Scarlet is. Have you seen her here tonight?"

"Um…yeah," she said. "Unfortunately."

Caleb narrowed his eyes.

"What does that mean?"

"Last I saw her, she was like in the process of stealing my boyfriend," she said.

Caleb narrowed his eyes further, trying to understand. Was Maria drunk, too?

"Is she here?" Caleb asked.

"No. She left a while ago."

"Do you know where?"

"No clue. And glad I don't."

"She's not responding to any of my calls or texts. Can you text her for me? I need to know where she is."

Maria hesitated.

"I'm sorry Mr. Paine, I'd like to help you. But after tonight, Scarlet and me are no longer friends. Sorry. I wouldn't text her if my life depended on it. In fact, I already deleted her from my contacts."

She turned and stormed away, back into the house, leaving Caleb more puzzled than he was before. At least he knew that Scarlet had been here. And that she had left. Possibly with some boy. And not Blake.

He wracked his brain for where to go next, and the more he thought about it, the more he realized the best place to wait was at home. After all, he didn't know where else to look, and eventually she had to come home.

Didn't she?

CHAPTER FOURTEEN

Scarlet pulled up to her house in Sage's growling Lamborghini, and parked it in the driveway. It had been the first time she had ever driven any car alone, and the whole ride had been terrifying, as she worried the whole way home that she'd get pulled over. She also felt especially funny driving this car, which was so expensive and which wasn't even hers.

She saw the empty house, her mom and dad's cars gone, and realized she was the only one home. She wondered where they could be at this late hour.

She glanced down at her phone as she turned off the car, and saw all the missed calls and texts from them. She felt guilty. She hadn't wanted to avoid them, but she knew they'd be furious at her for sneaking out. They wouldn't understand, and answering their calls would have just made everything much worse. There was no way she could explain it to them without their freaking out.

She worried that maybe they were out there looking for her. She felt bad about that. But at the same time, she was relieved the house was empty: at least she wouldn't have to march in and face the fire. She could sneak back up to her room, close the door, and go to bed. Maybe, if she left early enough in the morning, she to get to school without having to deal with them either. Give them time to cool off.

As Scarlet entered the house she was immediately greeted by Ruth, who jumped on her as she walked in. She knelt down and hugged her, kissing her, as Ruth licked her all over her face.

"I know Ruth," she said. "I missed you, too."

Scarlet walked from room to room and realized all the lights were on, as if her mom and dad had left in a rush.

"Hello?" she called out, just in case one of them was home by some chance.

No response.

Scarlet took out her phone and stared, thinking. If her parents were out there looking for her, she figured she should at least let them know she was home, so that they would come back and stop worrying. She could still go to bed before they got back.

She typed a quick text to them both:

Am home. Sorry I didn't text earlier. Going to bed now. See you tomorrow. Good night.

She sent it then powered it off so she wouldn't feel it buzzing and vibrating with their angry responses, which she was sure would come instantaneously.

She felt too wound up to go right to bed, and needed something to help her relax. She figured she had a quick ten minutes before her parents got home, and decided to make herself a cup of tea. She headed into the kitchen, Ruth at her heels, and put a pot of boiling water on the stove. She reached into the cabinet for a cup and teabag, and while she was at it, grabbed a treat and threw it to Ruth.

Ruth snatched the bone in midair, then carried it to the corner and started to chew.

Scarlet took her tea and walked with it into the small reading room at the side of the house, her favorite room, Ruth following. It was small and quirky, lined with books from floor to ceiling

She sat in the comfortable, overstuffed chair in the corner, set down her cup of tea on the coffee table and leaned back and closed her eyes, breathing deeply. As she closed her eyes, she heard the piano music Sage had played; she quickly tried to push it from her mind.

It had been a crazy day and night. The party. All the drama with Blake, and Vivian, and Maria. And Sage…. She felt a knot in her stomach as she contemplated what tomorrow might bring.

Most of all, she thought of Sage, of their magical time together, of his beautiful home, of his patio, and the moonlight, and the river.

And, of course, their first kiss. It was the most magical kiss she'd ever had. She could not stop thinking about it.

But then her mind turned to thoughts of Sage's asking her to leave. It had been so unexpected. She didn't understand. She knew she should be more understanding, but she wasn't. She really wanted answers. Was he rejecting her? Was there something wrong with her? With him? Why was he being so mysterious? Why couldn't he just tell her?

Scarlet sighed as she opened her eyes and took another sip of tea. Boys. Her drama with them never seemed to end.

As Scarlet scanned the room, she noticed something, on the far end. It was a book she had never seen before, sitting on the end table, beside the other reading chair. It had unusual look to it, and it dew her in. It looked like one of her mom's rare books, but it was smaller. Almost like…a journal.

Intrigued, she crossed the room, picked it up and examined it. She ran her hands along its worn edges, and as she turned the cover, the first page crinkled so loudly, she felt as if she were holding an ancient text. She had seen some of her mom's rare books before—but never anything like this.

As she read the first page, she was puzzled. She looked closer, and read it again and again. She couldn't understand. It looked like her mom's handwriting. Was this hers?

As she was reading the text, suddenly, her heart stopped. She could not believe what she was reading. What was this? Some kind of journal?

Scarlet realized this was her mom's journal, and a part of her told her it was private and she should put it down. But another part of her had to know. She read and read, knowing that she shouldn't.

It was definitely her mom's. Caitlin's journal. But this was not the Caitlin she knew. This was Caitlin as a young girl. As a teenager. She was mesmerized, turning the pages. It talked of falling in love with a man named Caleb. Having a daughter named Scarlet. Of becoming a vampire.

Her mom. A vampire. Changing. Transforming. Having hunger pangs. A sensitivity to light. Super strength. Wanting to feed on others. Just like her.

Scarlet's heart was pounding in her throat as she thought of herself. She remembered the other day, with Blake, by the river. She had felt it. Was it real? Was this the reason? Had her mom known all along? Was that was she was not telling her?

Scarlet turned the final page and saw a handwritten note, on a new piece of paper, taped to the back. It read:

"Must stop Scarlet."

Her heart pounded as she read it. What did that mean? Stop Scarlet? Stop her from doing what?

And that was when Scarlet realized: stop her from feeding. From transforming. From becoming a vampire.

There was only one way to do that: to kill her.

Scarlet felt her whole body go icy cold. She could not believe it: her own mom wanted to kill her.

Suddenly the front door banged open, and Scarlet jumped and dropped the book to the floor, knocking over her tea. She hurried into the living room and there, scowling down at her, was her dad.

"What the hell do you think you're doing!?" he screamed at her.

She was taken aback: she had never heard him use that tone of voice before, and had never seen him look so angry.

"Whose car is that?" he demanded, before she could even answer. "In the driveway? Who? Is he here? In the house? Where is he?"

"No one's here," she shot back. "I drove it back myself."

"You? What do you mean? You're not even licensed? Do you realize that?"

"I had no choice," she said, her mind reeling, feeling on the verge of tears.

"No choice? What are you talking about? Who owns that car?"

"A friend of mine," she said. "He let me borrow it."

"Let you borrow it? Who loans someone a Lamborghini? Is it one of your drug dealing friends?"

Drug dealing friends? What was he talking about? Scarlet wondered. *Had he lost his mind?*

"I don't have any drug-dealing friends," she said.

"Oh no?" he yelled. "Like Blake? He's not a drug dealer?"

"I don't even know what you're talking about," she yelled back, preparing in her mind to leave.

"How could you have lied to us? How could you have snuck out like that? Do you know how worried sick I was about you? I've been calling and texting you for hours. Why didn't you respond? What's gotten into you?"

"Because I knew you wouldn't understand!" she yelled.

"I understand everything," he snapped. "Too well. I know all about your pot smoking. Blake told me all about it."

Scarlet narrowed her eyes, wondering what he was talking about.

"You saw Blake?" she asked, surprised.

"I did," he said, "I went to the Wilsons. I saw him and I made it clear that he is never to see you again."

Scarlet reeled at his words. She couldn't believe it: her dad had gone to the party. He had shown up in front of everyone. He had confronted her ex-boyfriend. How humiliating. Now, she'd never be able to go back to school.

She was furious at her dad; she couldn't stand the sight of him. She didn't know who was worse—her mom, who wanted to kill her, or her dad, who wanted to humiliate her in front of everyone and who didn't even trust her.

She'd had enough. She marched through the living room and grabbed her coat off the rack.

"And where do you think you're going?" Caleb yelled, as he hurried over and grabbed her by the arm.

"Get off me!" she yelled.

But his grip was so strong, she wasn't going anywhere.

Scarlet had had enough: in a flash, she was suddenly overwhelmed by a surge of rage. It rose up throughout her body, like a flash of heat, taking over. Without even meaning to, she turned and snarled at Caleb.

"I said get OFF of me!" she snarled.

She spun and shook her arm free with a strength she didn't even know she had, then shoved him. She barely touched him, but as she did, he went flying across the room, crashing into the dining table and knocking it over.

He sat there, on the floor, looking up at her, blinking in stunned silence.

Scarlet knew that this was the moment that changed everything.

She was done with this house. Done with her parents. It was time for her to leave here—and to never come back.

CHAPTER FIFTEEN

Scarlet raced in the Lamborghini, speeding down the twisting and turning side streets, still trembling from her encounter with her dad. She had been shocked by his anger, and even more shocked at her own reaction. She hadn't meant to hurt him like that; she'd only wanted to throw his arm off, to shove him away. She had barely touched him, and he'd gone flying across the room, like a cannonball. She had never seen anything like it, and her own strength terrified her.

Was it true? Was everything in her mom's journal real?

Was she becoming a vampire?

Scarlet was finding it harder and harder to discount all of the strange things happening to her. Her super strength. The light sensitivity. Her speed. And most of all, her desire to feed. Too many things were adding up.

As she drove in the darkness, she felt there was only one place she could go, only one person she could turn to who might understand.

Sage.

She didn't know why, especially after his having asked her to leave, but for some reason she felt he'd understand. She followed the streets back to River Road, past mansion after mansion, until she came to his.

Her heart was pounding as she pulled through the open gates, onto his driveway. Was coming here a mistake?

She didn't know where else to go, and felt as if she had no one else left in the world. If all that drama hadn't happened tonight, maybe she could crash with Maria. But after tonight, that wasn't an option.

She sped down his driveway, pulled up before the door and killed the ignition, amazed she made it in his car in one piece.

She jumped out and marched to front door, her footsteps crunching on the gravel, and as she did, she was struck with a terrible thought: what if Sage didn't want her here after all? What if he sent her away? She would be crushed. And then, where would she go? After all, just hours ago, he had told her to leave. Might her showing up here like this turn him off?

She just needed a place to stay. Even if he didn't want to see her anymore, maybe he could just let her crash on a couch somewhere, just give her until the morning to figure things out. After all, his house was big enough.

She took a deep breath as she reached for the knocker.

But as she did, the door suddenly opened.

Standing there, facing her, was a boy she'd never met. He looked to be about Sage's build, except he was taller, with sandy, long-ish hair, and blue eyes. He was very attractive, but there was something about him—something almost sinister—that Scarlet sensed right away. Her skin went cold in his presence.

"Well, you must be Scarlet," he said, a smile on his face, as he extended his hand.

She shook it warily, and felt a dark energy emanating off of it as she did. Her hand had never felt so cold. His eyes seemed to gleam, to light up as he touched her. She didn't understand how he knew her name—had Sage been talking about her?

"I'm Lore," he said. "Sage's cousin."

"Nice to meet you," she said.

He held onto her hand too long, and as he stared down at her, his eyes locking on hers, she began to feel a little creeped out.

"I've heard so much about you," he added.

"You have?" she asked, hearing the surprise in her own voice. Had Sage really been talking about her? She hoped that he had.

"All the time," he said. "Seems our boy is smitten. Though he'd never admit it. But don't flatter yourself just yet—he's that way with every girl that comes around."

Scarlet's heart sank. Was he telling the truth? Somehow she doubted he was.

"Um…is Sage here?" she asked.

Suddenly Sage appeared in the door, reaching out with one arm and pushing Lore side. She sensed the tension between them.

"Well then," Lore said with a smile, and disappeared into the house.

"Sorry about him," Sage said.

"Who is he?" she asked. "Is that really your cousin?" She suddenly started to worry if his family was really creeped out.

"He is. It's a long story," Sage said.

He looked down at the car keys in her hand, and she realized, and reached out and handed them to him.

"I'm sorry to come back," she said.

"I'm glad you did," he said with a smile. His words warmed her heart. She knew it. She knew he'd understand. Finally, a place in the world where she was welcome.

"Sorry about before," he added. "It wasn't me. It was just…" He looked away. "I can't really explain it."

She could feel he was genuine, and didn't want to bring it up again.

"Don't worry," she said. "I understand. Maybe it was all just a bit much at once."

She sensed movement inside the house. Sage must've sensed it, too, because he stepped outside and closed the door behind them.

"It's a nice night," he said. "Let's take a walk."

She was happy as she reached out and placed her hand in his. It felt good to hold his hand again, and he led her for a walk on the grounds, around the side of the house.

They followed a winding trail that led them around the backyard, then twisted and turned off to the side of the house, underneath huge trees. It led them across the rolling grounds, up and down hills beneath the huge full moon.

"There's so much about me that I want to tell you," he said, after they'd walked for a while in silence. "But I can't."

"Why can't you?" she asked.

He looked away, sighing.

"It's a family thing," he said. "I'm sworn to secrecy. It's hard to explain."

She wanted to know more, of course, but she didn't want to pry. She was just happy to be here with him.

"It's okay," she said. "I'm just happy to be with you."

"I'm so happy you came back," he said with a smile.

She turned and smiled at him as they walked. She had never been happier. She wanted him to know everything about her.

"I had some drama with my parents," she said. "It's…well, um, I guess it's kind of hard for me to explain, too," she said, trying to think of how much to tell him. She didn't want to sound crazy. "Sometimes I feel like no one understands me," she said. "Sometimes I feel like I don't even understand myself. The last few days…they've been so crazy. I don't know how to explain it. But I…I feel like I'm changing…"

He turned and looked at her.

"What do you mean, changing?"

She struggled in her mind over how much to tell him. She didn't want to scare him away; but at the same time, she was beginning to feel really close to him, and a part of her felt that she had to lay it all out on the line now, upfront, before their relationship could get any deeper. She wanted him to know, wanted him to either reject or accept her for what she was. If her heart was going to get broken, she'd rather it get broken now.

The trail rounded a bend and finally sloped down, right to the bank of the Hudson. They reached the shore, and stood on the sand, looking out at the water, which was aglow in the moonlight.

"I know this sounds crazy," she said. "And if you think I'm crazy, just tell me. But these last few days…my body…well…I can't deny it anymore. I'm different. I'm not the person I was. I can't explain it, I know this sounds insane but…I think I'm becoming a vampire."

Scarlet turned and looked into his eyes, searching for his response, expecting him to send her away. Her heart was pounding as she hoped and prayed that he wouldn't.

But to her surprise, his expression hardly changed. Almost as if he'd expected this.

"I don't think that's crazy at all," he said.

She stared back at him.

"You *don't?*" she asked, shocked.

He shook his head.

"The other day," she continued, excited to be able to tell someone, "I had this urge, it was so strong. I haven't told anyone. But like, when I was with Blake, I felt this need to, like, feed on him. Like, drink his blood. I'm sorry, I know that sounds gross. But I can't deny it. I really did. Not that I understand it. I was afraid it might happen with you. But the weird thing is, when I'm around you, I don't get that urge. I don't understand that, either. Am I losing my mind?"

He turned and stared at her.

"It makes sense to me. All of it. And if you knew more about me, you'd understand why."

Now Scarlet was intrigued; she felt a sudden to urge know everything about him.

"Please tell me," she asked. "Please. I need to know."

Sage turned and looked up at his house; he looked as if he were in fear of something. He turned and searched the shore, and his eyes locked on a small canoe, nestled against the water.

"I will," he said. "But not here. Do you like boats?"

Boats? she wondered.

"See that small island out there?" he asked, pointing.

She looked out and saw a small, uninhabited island in the middle of the river, covered in trees.

"I visit it sometimes. What do you say? It's a beautiful night. When we get there, when it's just the two of us, surrounded by water, I'll tell you everything."

He held out a hand.

Scarlet smiled as she placed her hand in his. There was nothing she wanted more in the world.

CHAPTER SIXTEEN

Scarlet stepped into the narrow, rocking kayak as Sage held it steady for her. He followed her in, then shoved off from shore.

They went gliding, weightless, into the strong tides of the Hudson River.

The huge moon sat on the horizon, lighting up the water, and the night was incredibly still. The only sound Scarlet could hear was the lapping of the waves against the boat.

She leaned back in the boat and closed her eyes, feeling the water gently rock her, as Sage paddled the kayak, alternating hands. She breathed in the cool, moist October air coming off the river, and for the first time in a while, felt completely at ease in the world.

She opened her eyes and looked up, and saw a galaxy filled with stars. It was the most magical night she'd ever seen.

They soon approached a small island, sitting in the middle of the Hudson. Uninhabited, covered in trees, it stretched hardly a hundred feet in each direction and was ringed by a small, sandy shore.

"I come out here sometimes," Sage said softly in the night. "It's a place I can go to be alone. I've never shared it with anyone."

She was touched.

"Thanks for bringing me."

They lodged on its narrow shore, and Sage jumped out and pulled the boat up onto the sand. He then reached out and gave Scarlet a hand up.

Sage yanked the boat further onto the sand, making sure it was secure, then reached down and took off his shoes. Scarlet did the same, and the sand felt so nice and cool on her bare feet.

He took her hand and led her across the small beach, bringing her to a spot halfway around the island, marked by a sand dune. They sat side by side. She leaned back against the sandy dune, and had never been so comfortable. It was like reclining back into a chair.

Above their heads were the branches of a tree, leaning out over the river. Before her, the entire Hudson was spread out.

He reached over and took her hand in his, interlacing their fingers. Their hands felt as if they were meant for each other.

They sat in silence for a long time, and Scarlet began to wonder if he was ever going to speak. She hoped that he would. She loved just sitting there like this, but she was dying to know everything him. Her mind raced with questions. But she thought it best to wait until he was ready to tell her whatever it was he wanted to.

She didn't know how much more time had passed, when finally, he cleared his throat.

"I'm going to tell you everything," he began. "But you have to promise to keep it a secret."

She looked over and saw how serious he was.

"I promise," she said earnestly. "You can trust me. After all, I trusted you: I just told you I thought I was a vampire."

"But what I might tell you, it might turn you away," he said. "If that's what you decide, then I understand." He looked down. "You probably won't believe me when I tell you."

"Sage, I promise," she said. "I'll believe you. Whatever it is, I'll believe you."

He looked up into her eyes, and he finally seemed to believe her. He looked back down at the water for a very long time, until once again, he was ready to talk.

"I am an Immortalist. I come from a family of Immortalists. We have been alive for nearly two thousand years. Our name, though, is deceptive: we are not immortal. None of us. Our life span is finite. Two thousand years, exactly. In fact, as fate would have it, we have only weeks left to live."

Scarlet felt a knife go through her heart. He would die in a few weeks?

She stared back at him, her heart pounding with the ramifications. She wanted desperately to believe him. And a part of her did. It would explain everything—how different he was, how different his family was. Why she felt so strongly about him.

"You're going to die?" she asked, barely able to say the words.

He nodded.

"That's why I had to send you away earlier," he explained. "I got struck by the pains. In our final months, the pains get worse. I didn't want you to see me like that. And I didn't know how to explain."

"But you could have just told me," she said, her heart lifting as she finally realized that he hadn't been rejecting her after all. "I would have understood."

"Would you have?" he asked, staring at her.

Scarlet thought about it, and realized that maybe he was right, maybe she wouldn't have understood. Maybe at the time it would have all seemed too far-fetched, too fantastical. She wasn't even entirely sure if she believed all of it now. A part of her still wondered if this was all just Sage's strange fantasy.

"You are wondering," he said, looking at her. "I can sense it. You don't believe me."

"Well, I, um…well, it's not that I don't believe you…it's just that…"

"I'll show you," he said, suddenly sitting up. "I'll prove it to you. Give me your hand."

She looked at him skeptically.

"You don't have to prove anything," she said.

"I want to," he said. "I want you to believe me. To truly believe me. It's important to me."

He held out his hand, palm down, and she slowly placed hers under his, palm up, wondering.

He closed his eyes, and as he did, she felt a tremendous heat emanating from his palm. The heat grew more and more intense, until he opened his eyes and slowly removed his hand.

As he did, she was shocked at what she saw: sitting there, in her palm, was a small, translucent orb, a circular white light about the size of a baseball. It was warm and fuzzy to the touch. She was amazed to see it rise up and hover just over her palm.

"What is it?" she asked, breathless.

"A light orb," he explained.

"What does it do?" she asked in wonder.

"We use them to light up the night, or sometimes for heat, or for healing. Sometimes, we use them just for fun, the same way your kind blow bubbles. We send them off into the night, like balloons. Eventually, they dissipate. Watch."

He bent over and blew on her hand, and as he did, she was amazed to watch the orb drift off into the air. It flew in the air, carried by the wind, like a balloon. She watched as it floated over the Hudson, slowly getting farther and farther away, like a firefly disappearing into the night.

She hardly knew what to say. She couldn't believe it: it was real. All of this was real. Every word Sage was saying was true. The supernatural really did exist. Which meant, maybe, she was a vampire. And which meant Sage really was going to die soon. These thoughts overwhelmed her.

"We have our own strengths and vulnerabilities," he continued. "For example, we have super-sonic hearing, yet we cannot hear over bodies of water. We cannot tolerate high-pitched sounds, which can incapacitate us. We don't need to feed—ever. Our own life force is self-sustaining. That is why we've been able to live in harmony with humans all this time. Yet, despite this, some of our kind do feed anyway. Not because they have to, but because they get a high from it. Feeding on a human gives a rush, like a drug high. It has been outlawed by our Grand Council and is strictly forbidden. Lack of harmony with humans is bad for us all, and can draw unwanted attention. But now, with the end of days coming, everything is changing. The rules are being disregarded."

He took a deep breath.

"We don't have blood. And that is why you felt no urge to feed on me, as you had with Blake. Vampires are more powerful than humans, but we are more powerful than vampires."

Scarlet's heart was pounding, as she was starting to believe it all. He was so convincing.

"We have the ability to transform into a raven-like creature," he added. "When we choose to, we can fly. When our kind feeds on humans, they swoop down and wrap their wings around a human tightly. It doesn't kill them. But it does drain their energy and can lead to a psychotic break."

Scarlet suddenly realized.

"Tina. That girl in my class. The one who was attacked by an animal the other night and went crazy. One of yours did that?"

Sage nodded back gravely.

"Lore. I am ashamed to say. He's out of control."

Scarlet's mind spun as she tried to process it all. She didn't feel afraid of Sage, but she sensed danger, and was growing increasingly afraid.

"Is that why your family came here? To this town? To feed?"

"It's more complicated than that," he said. "They didn't come to feed. Not most of them, anyway. They came for the cure."

"The cure?" she asked, perplexed.

"Our legend tells us there is a cure for our condition, an elixir that will enable us to live past our two thousand year limit. One that will enable us to be truly immortal."

"And you think the cure is here?" she asked.

"My family does. Legend tells us there will come a day when there appears one other immortal being on our planet. A teenage girl. A vampire. And that she will hold the key. She must give us this key freely in order for it to work. Once we have it, it will lead us to the elixir. And then, we will be cured. And truly immortal."

Scarlet's eyes lit up in recognition. She was almost afraid to ask.

"The teenage girl. The vampire. Is that…me?"

"Yes," he said, gravely. "It is."

Scarlet started shaking inside. She felt her whole world crumbling around her. So that was why Sage was interested in her. Not because he liked her. But only because he thought she held the key to his immortality. She felt hurt. Used.

"So," she said, devastated, "then that's it? The reason you're with me? Just so you can get the key and live forever?"

She felt like crying, and began to get up to leave.

Sage sat up and grabbed hold of her wrist.

"Scarlet, it's not like that. You have to understand. Please, give me a chance."

She saw the earnestness in his eyes, and willed herself to listen. To give him one chance.

"It's true, my parents sent me on this mission, to come to the school, to meet you. They were hoping I would convince you to give us the key. Yes, it's true, they hoped I would gain your trust. At first, I went along with the mission."

He leaned in and looked at her meaningfully.

"But from the moment I met you, I knew I could never go through with it. I knew from the second I saw you that I loved you too much. This, now, our being together—it has nothing to do with their mission. It has everything to do with us. That is *their* mission, not mine. I'm here with you now because I love you."

Scarlet examined his face, searching it to see if he was being honest. She sensed that he was.

He *loved* her. She could hardly believe it. Especially because she felt that she loved him, too.

"I know it's too soon to use such strong words. But I say what I feel. I always have. And I have only weeks left to live. I am have no time to waste. I want you to know how I feel. I *need* for you to know how I feel."

Scarlet saw the sincerity in his eyes, and she believed him. And she loved him back, more than ever. But at the same time, her heart was breaking.

"I mean, why fall in love with me? Why now?" she asked, on the verge of tears. "When you only have weeks left to live? Why torture yourself? Why torture me?"

"I know," he said. "And I am sorry. I didn't plan on this."

The thought of his death pained her terribly. She couldn't lose him.

"I don't understand," she said. "Why can't I just give you the key? I mean, I don't even know what it is, but if I have it, why can't I just hand it to you? I don't want to see you die."

He shook his head.

"You don't understand. It's not that simple. Yes, you do have the key. I have seen it. In fact, I see it right now."

Scarlet saw him look down at her throat, and she suddenly realized.

Her necklace. The one her mom had given her. The one that the priest had freaked out about. That was his key. That was what they wanted.

"Just take it," she said, reaching back to unclasp it.

He reached up and grabbed her wrist, stopping her.

"I will not," he said firmly. "In order for our elixir to work, in order for our kind to be immortal, there are two steps. The first is that they must use the key, find the elixir and drink. The second is that they must kill the key-giver."

Scarlet looked at him, and her eyes widened in horror.

"I'm sorry," he added softly. "Legend has it there can only be one immortal creature on earth. That is what they believe. And that is why I cannot accept the key."

He stared off into the river, as she collected her thoughts. Her mind was spinning

"That is why I've been lying to my family," he said. "I don't trust them. They are desperate. They will stop at nothing to get your key. And to kill you. That is why I brought you here, to this island. To be safe from them. The water, it protects us from their watchful ears. Not all of my kind are as caring: if I don't bring back the necklace, they will try to kill you."

He reached out and slid a small ring on her index finger. It shined even in the night, covered with diamonds and rubies and sapphires. All along its gold band were ancient symbols. It looked priceless. She was amazed as it slid on her finger: it fit perfectly.

"This will protect you from them," he said. "If one of them ever tries to attack you, this will save you."

"But there's still one thing I don't understand," she said, feeling on the verge of tears. "If I don't give you my necklace, you'll die. By saving me, you're allowing yourself to die. You would rather die yourself than see me dead? Why? You don't even know me."

He looked down, then looked up, his eyes filled with tears.

"You're right. I don't know you. But I do love you. And I would happily give up my life for you. I know it sounds crazy. But that's how I feel."

Scarlet was overwhelmed with emotion. She hardly knew what to say. She'd never met anyone as intense as Sage. And never met anyone who loved her as much. It was crazy. But somehow, she understood. Somehow, she felt the same amount of love for him. And she didn't want him to die.

She reached up and took off her necklace and pushed it into his palm.

"I don't want you to die," she said, crying. "Please. Take it."

He pushed it back into her palm, as his eyes welled up.

"I'm sorry," he said. "But I never would."

Scarlet leaned in and embraced Sage, and he hugged her back. She hugged him tightly, not wanting to let him go, overwhelmed with grief, love, longing. Anger at fate. She couldn't understand why the world had brought them together only to tear them apart. She clung to him, crying, willing for the universe to change their destiny—and knowing somehow that it would not. As he hugged her back, his muscles rippling, she felt so safe in his arms, and yet so sad, knowing that in just a few weeks, she would never be in those arms again.

Did fate have to be so cruel?

CHAPTER SEVENTEEN

Caitlin sat in the back of the foreign taxi as it wound its way through the narrow streets of Paris in the pouring rain. It had been a long, rough taxi ride from the airport, and she hadn't slept a wink on the plane. She had dozed off once or twice, but to fast, rapid nightmares which forced her to wake instantly, determined not to fall asleep again.

Now she was exhausted as they went block to block, combing the streets, searching for the bookstore. It was daybreak, and she could barely see out the window. They had been circling this small group of blocks for nearly an hour now, and Caitlin was beginning to feel hopeless. She'd been arguing back and forth with the taxi driver, he speaking French and she English, and neither understanding each other.

"Six rue Charlemagne!" Caitlin yelled again, enunciating each syllable.

He screamed something back in French, which she did not understand. They were both at the end of each other's ropes.

As they circled the block yet again, she looked out and again caught a glimpse of the sign. Clearly, this was the right street. Then she watched the numbers, saw them climb from one to ten. But for some reason, there was no number six. She couldn't understand it. They had been around this block again and again, with always the same result. She knew it was the right block—there was no other block by this name in Paris. It *had* to be it. Maybe she was just missing it from the back of the taxicab. She had no choice. She had to get out and see for herself.

"Pull over!" she yelled out.

She paid the driver, gathered her briefcase and jumped out of the cab into the pouring rain. The rain came down in sheets, and she hadn't brought an umbrella. In seconds, she was soaked.

Caitlin ran down the deserted, cobblestone block, taking shelter beneath an awning jutting out from one of the old buildings. She stood flush against the wall, just barely getting out of the rain, and wiped the water from her hair and eyes. She looked down at the handwritten street name and number again, but now the ink was running with water.

She put it away. No matter. She'd memorized the address. Six rue Charlemagne.

Caitlin looked out and from where she was standing and scrutinized the numbers on all the buildings. She was on the even side of the street—it had to be on the other side.

She ran out into the rain, everything so loud from the pouring water, getting completely doused again, and crossed over to the other side of the street. She peered closely at the numbers. She saw an eight, but no six. As she looked closely, though, she realized she'd overlooked something: a tiny, narrow staircase, leading down. Between the buildings. On the door, below street level, was a faded number. She peered carefully, and her heart fluttered. Six.

There was no storefront, but then again, that made sense: the old lady wanted no visitors.

Caitlin took two steps down, reached out, grabbed the ancient lion's head knocker, and slammed it several times against the door. The sound reverberated in the empty block.

Caitlin stood there and looked at her watch: 6 AM local time. Aiden had warned her that the woman may not answer, even if she were in. But now, at this time of day, in this weather, what were the odds?

Caitlin had a sinking feeling this would not go well. She couldn't stand to contemplate her options: she had crossed half the world for this, and the woman might not even answer.

Caitlin slammed the knocker again and again, her clothes completely soaked as she stood there. After several more minutes of waiting, she finally turned and examined the streets, looking for any sign of a café, any place where she could wait, and rest, and get a cup of coffee, and warm up. But all the storefronts were closed this time of day, their gates down. There wasn't a soul in sight.

Caitlin stood there, shivering, wondering what to do next. Suddenly, to her shock, she heard a noise at the door. There was the sound of several heavy bolts unlocking, and to her amazement, the door opened.

There stood a small, petite woman, who looked to be in her 90s. She stood there proudly, standing erect, staring up at Caitlin disapprovingly with her sea-blue French eyes. They looked as if they'd witness the creation of the world.

The old woman snapped at her. It was something in French, which Caitlin did not understand.

"I'm sorry," Caitlin replied. "But I don't speak French."

The woman merely stared back, cooly.

Caitlin worried she might close the door, and thought quick.

"I'm a friend of Aiden's. He sent me here," she said in a rush.

The woman stared back coolly, expressionless, with a slight frown.

Then, suddenly, she took a half step back, and began to shut the door.

Caitlin could not believe it. She was not going to let her in.

Desperate, she stepped forward and stuck her foot in the crack before the door could close.

"Please. You don't understand. I just traveled half the world to get here. I'm just a mother who loves her daughter very much. Who's concerned for her. You have a book I need. A very rare book. Please. I have nowhere else to turn."

The woman stared back at her for what felt like forever, then slowly, her expression softened. The woman looked warily both ways herself, then gestured her in.

Caitlin quickly hurried in from the pouring rain, and as she did, the woman slammed and locked the door behind her.

Caitlin stood there, in the low, arched-ceiling room, the rain slamming against the windows, and a puddle of water quickly forming beneath her feet on the ancient wood floors. She looked down, embarrassed.

"I'm so sorry," she said.

The old woman handed her something soft, and she realized: a towel. She was touched. She dried her hair, so grateful, then dried her face and neck.

"Take off your coat," the woman ordered.

Caitlin was shocked: she spoke English. And she cared.

Caitlin peeled off her dripping coat, and as she did, the woman placed another dry towel over her shoulders. Caitlin rubbed it, drying her shirt.

"Thank you," she said, so appreciative.

"It's warmer here," the woman said, as she led Caitlin to a small fireplace on the opposite side of the room, inside of which was a raging fire. Caitlin walked to it and held out her hands, relishing in its heat.

Caitlin looked around, surveying the cozy room. It was dimly lit by candle sconces and bedecked with rugs and cozy, antique sitting chairs. What caught her eye most, though, were the bookcases: she saw at a glance that there was an abundance of riches in this small room. She was astonished. It was a treasure trove of ancient, rare volumes. She felt as if she'd stepped back in time, to a lost world.

"I'm looking for a very rare volume," Caitlin said. "I'm not even certain it exists. Vairo's *De Fascino Libri Tres*. I am looking for the other half of a missing page."

Slowly, Caitlin reached into her bag and removed the folder and the torn page. She held it out, and the old woman's eyes widened just a bit as she examined it.

After a few moments, she handed it back to Caitlin.

"Do you know it?" Caitlin asked. "Do you have it?"

"Forty years ago, I took in a collection of the most obscure and rare editions of occult titles," the woman said, her voice scratchy and barely audible over the crackling fire. "I didn't want to, frankly, but my late husband insisted. I've never liked the energy off of those books. I walled them off, so that no one would ever know they were here. Including myself. I've had some very unsavory types come looking for them over the years. And I've always denied their existence."

The old woman suddenly crossed the room, reached up and pulled a light fixture on the far wall.

To Caitlin's amazement, the stone wall suddenly slid to the side, to the sound of stone scraping stone. It revealed a secret room.

The old woman stepped in, raised her candle, and lit several candles sconces inside the room. As she did, Caitlin could see that it was jam packed with rare books, stacks and stacks of them. There was barely room to walk.

"If I have what you're looking for," the old woman said, as she came back out and faced Caitlin, "it's in there."

If? Caitlin wondered. Her heart sank as she took in the room: it was massive. There were thousands and thousands of titles, all unorganized, throw in random heaps on the floor. Her professional eye told her it could take weeks to go through them all. She didn't have time.

"Do you have any idea at all if you have it?" Caitlin asked. "Do you have any idea at all where in this room it might be?"

The old woman shook her head.

"It was forty years ago," she said, "and even back then, I barely glanced at them. You're going to have to find out the hard way."

Caitlin took a few tentative steps into the room, ducking as she went beneath the low arched stone, and as she did, the woman turned to her.

"When you're done, knock three times."

With that, the old woman pulled the lever and suddenly, the door slid closed on Caitlin.

Caitlin stood there, amazed, scanning the mountains of books, and wondering what she had gotten herself into.

CHAPTER EIGHTEEN

Sage crossed his bedroom, gathering his things, packing up ancient artifacts he hadn't looked at in centuries. He was finally ready to leave this place, his family, for good. He had a large opened suitcase on his bed, and rifled through items, deciding what to let go. He held up a small ivory tusk off his desk, remembering when he had found it five hundred years before. He examined it, then set it down, deciding not to bring it.

As he stood there, by the window, he glanced out, and looked at the Hudson. In the early morning light the water sparkled. In the distance he saw the island he'd spent the night on with Scarlet, the two of them having fallen asleep, clothed, in each other's arms. It had been innocent, but the most beautiful night he had ever spent on this planet. He could not stop thinking about the moment they woke up together, watched the dawn break together, the sun rise over the Hudson. It had seemed to rise right over them, as if they were in the very center of the world.

Waking with Scarlet in his arms had given him a feeling of being restored that he hadn't had in years. It made him feel whole again, and it gave him, for the first time in a long time, a reason to live.

They had decided to run away together. Scarlet had decided it would be best to keep up appearances for now, to go back to school in the morning, to face all her friends, to see them one last time, and then for them to leave that night, in the cover of darkness. They made a plan to meet after school, at the big dance that night, and leave from there. They would leave this town, find some place in the world where they could be alone, away from their families, from everyone who wanted to tear them apart. There was nothing Sage wanted more: if these were to be his last few weeks on the planet, he wanted them to be worthy ones. He wanted to live for *himself* for a change.

Scarlet had even talked about the two of them taking off right then and there, at dawn. Sage had wanted to, too. But he thought it would be more prudent for them to leave at night, in the cover of darkness. Scarlet also wanted to have closure with her friends, and

Sage wanted a little bit of time to gather his things, and to internally say his goodbyes to his family. Of course, he could not tell him he was leaving. But maybe there was still a small chance he could convince them, get them to change their minds about Scarlet. After two thousand years together, they owed it to him to at least hear him out. If he was successful, maybe, just maybe, they would let her go, and the two of them could live out their final days here in peace.

Deep down, he knew it was a lost cause. His family's mortality was at stake, after all. They would, he knew, go after Scarlet with everything they had. After tonight, after his deadline was up, they would hunt her down and kill her.

So as a contingency plan, Sage gathered everything important from his room. He had a feeling that, after today, he would never be back here again. And that was okay with him. He would miss his family, after all this time, but he knew there wasn't much time left to live anyway, and he wanted to spend his final weeks how *he* wanted to spend them—not how his parents wanted him to spend them. Enough was enough. There were no punishments they could inflict on him now that would be worse than the punishment of not being able to spend time with Scarlet.

He hoped that Lore would not be foolish enough to try to attack Scarlet. After all, they all knew it would be useless to kill her without her voluntarily handing over the necklace. But they could be impetuous, especially Lore—and with just a few weeks left to live, who knew how they might react.

"You always were a hopeless romantic," came a voice.

Sage spun around and was surprised to see, standing there, his sister, Phoenicia.

She stood there, staring at him disapprovingly in the doorway, slowly shaking her head.

"Such a sap," she said. "Always have been."

And what are you? he thought. *Afraid to fall in love? You've had your guard up for centuries. Where has that gotten you?*

He ignored her, crossing the room, picking up a framed piece of sheet music, signed by Beethoven, and putting it into his backpack.

"You don't know what you're talking about," he said.

"Going somewhere?" she asked.

He pored over his bookcase, taking out a first edition of Shakespeare's *Macbeth* and inserting it into his bag.

Phoenicia suddenly crossed the room, reaching him with lightning speed, grabbed his wrist, and snatched the book from his hand. She slammed it down on the tabletop, and scowled at him.

"What the hell do you think you're doing?" she hissed.

Now he was annoyed. He frowned back.

"What business of it is yours?"

"Everything that you do is my business. Everything that goes on around here is my business. Especially now. You're so cavalier, as if nothing matters, as if we have all the time in the world. We're all counting on you. Have you forgotten? And here you are, in another one of your romantic escapades, as if you haven't a care in the world. You can fool mom and dad, but you can't fool me. I know you could care less about getting the key from her. I know that you've fallen in love with her. You don't care about any of us. You will die, and you don't care about that either, do you?"

He stared at her, his eyes narrowing as he felt a rage building. That was so like her. His entire life she had plagued him, always the first to point out his faults—or her perception of his faults. She was a cynic, that was her problem. She didn't believe in love at all.

Sage had given up trying to answer her centuries ago. She would never understand anything when it came to love.

Especially now. How could she possibly understand about Scarlet? How could he explain to her the way Scarlet made him feel? The way she looked in the morning light? Her grace? Her sensitivity? Her kindness? He could barely understand it all himself.

"I don't know what you want me to say," he said.

"I want you to say that you will get the key. That you will do it now!"

She stared back at him with intensity, but he slowly shook his head.

"It's a myth," he said. "Don't you see? We're destined to die. All of us. Our destiny has always been two thousand years. And nothing we can do will change that. Attacking some poor girl is not going to change your life."

She narrowed her eyes.

"You wouldn't be trying to protect her unless you thought it was all true. That she really was the one." She narrowed her eyes further. "I'll be that she even offered you the key already—and that you said no. You did, didn't you?"

He looked at her, blushing. It was uncanny how she could always read him.

"What do you care?" he said. "What are you going to do? Kill me? We're all dying anyway."

She shook her head in disappointment, and as she did, suddenly he saw something he had never seen before, in all his centuries of knowing her: a tear forming at the corner of her eye.

"After all this time, do you even care at all about me? Or yourself?"

He softened, feeling bad, and realizing he couldn't lie to her anymore.

"Phoenicia. You're my sister. I love you. I really do. But I'm sorry. She's worth all of it and more to me."

Phoenicia narrowed her eyes in anger.

"Is this girl, this stranger, worth even more than me?"

Her face reddened as she turned and stormed out the room and slammed the door behind her.

Sage knew that wherever she was going, trouble would soon follow.

CHAPTER NINETEEN

Scarlet walked through her high school halls in a daze, hardly aware of where she was. She felt as if she were walking on air. She couldn't stop re-living her night with Sage; his energy still lingered with every step she took. For the first time, she was hardly bothered by all the kids around her, swarming in every direction, she could barely hear the noise. She didn't even care. Because now, for the first time she could remember, her heart was full. She was madly in love with Sage. Completely obsessed with him.

Her feelings for Sage were so overwhelming, she could hardly think of anything else. She felt it like a shield, hovering around her, protecting her. It felt like now, nothing could get to her. With Sage by her side, she felt invincible.

And soon enough, tonight, the two of them would take off, get away from here, away from her parents, her friends and all their petty drama, to a world of their own. To a place where they could be together, without anyone trying to get between them. All she had to do was get through this day, make it to tonight, to the dance, where Sage would meet her, and they would leave together. Her heart was pounding with anticipation; she already couldn't wait for the day to end.

The bell rang, and she glanced at her phone as she headed towards her English class. She saw all the missed calls and texts from her dad, and cringed. She hardly knew how to respond, and couldn't deal with it right now. She also noticed that Maria hadn't texted or called. As she headed to their joint class, she braced herself for her reaction.

Scarlet entered the classroom just in time. It was already filled and she noticed immediately that her customary seat, next to Maria, was taken. She couldn't believe it: Maria always made sure that seat was reserved for her. Now, some other kid was sitting in it. Maria, sitting in her usual seat, didn't even look over at her. It felt like a betrayal, and it was a clear message: Maria didn't want Scarlet sitting next to her. This did not bode well.

Scarlet hurried down the row, and as she did, Maria glanced at her, then pointedly looked away.

Scarlet walked past her, feeling hurt. On the one hand, she understood. From Maria's perspective, Scarlet had stolen Sage away. But that wasn't true, and it wasn't fair. Sage had never liked Maria; Scarlet had even tried to set them up, and he just didn't like her.

Scarlet felt that Maria should realize that, and that the way she was acting just wasn't fair. She was living in a fantasy. Sage would've ended up with someone else, whether it was Scarlet or not.

But Maria could be so possessive and territorial and jealous that if anyone ever even talked to anyone she remotely liked, she took it as a personal insult. For Maria, this was like a nuclear bomb. Scarlet hoped that she would be big enough to get over it, because Scarlet wasn't going to let Sage go. But clearly, Maria was not budging. This time, it was bad. In all the years she had known her, she had never seen Maria like this, so furious at her. Scarlet had a sinking feeling that this would be the end of their relationship.

The thought saddened Scarlet as she took her seat in the back row, set down her books, and turned and looked out the window. If that was how Maria wanted it, then that was how it would be. After all, after tonight, Scarlet wouldn't be here anymore anyway. Soon, none of this would matter anymore. Soon, she would be with Sage, far away from here.

"Okay class, please open to Act Five, Scene Three of *Romeo and Juliet*," Mr. Sparrow said. "The famous tomb scene. Show of hands: how many of you read this last night?"

A few hesitant hands rose.

"Very good. So then you will know what I'm talking about."

Scarlet zoned out, as her thoughts turned back to Sage. She thought again of last night, of all that he told her, of who he was, who his family was. She remembered that orb he had created, in her palm, remembered watching it float away. She believed him. It was obvious, he was not like anybody else. And she felt in her heart that the two of them were meant to be together. Two immortals. Two different types of creatures. Unlike anyone else on earth. They were destined for each other.

Most of all, he understood her. He didn't make fun of her when she said she was a vampire; he understood. He wasn't even surprised. And he wasn't afraid. For the first time, it made Scarlet feel comfortable in her own skin, in who she was becoming. It also made her feel greatly relieved that she could be around Sage without wanting to feed on him.

But Scarlet then thought of Sage's limited life span, of his few weeks left to live, and she felt overwhelmed with sadness. It wasn't fair. To find the love of her life, and only have a few weeks to be with him—it just wasn't fair.

"And that is what makes this play different," the teacher announced. "Romeo and Juliet each decide to die for each other. Without their love, they feel that life is not worth living. They are just from two very different families. Families that want to tear them apart. When all they want is to love each other."

Scarlet looked up, paying attention to Mr. Sparrow's words for the first time. She looked up at the lines he'd written on the board:

O happy dagger! This is thy sheath; there rust, and let me die.

"Juliet's last words, as she kills herself with Romeo's dagger. That is what makes it a love story. Their sacrifice. How many of us are willing to sacrifice like this for love? Will any of us ever encounter a love this great?"

Scarlet thought about that. Romeo had given up his life for Juliet's; Juliet had given up her life for Romeo. Shouldn't she give Sage her necklace? Why was her life worth more than his?

The class sat there, in silence, when suddenly the bell rang.

As everyone headed for the door, Scarlet noticed Maria hurry out faster than the others, clearly wanting to avoid her. Scarlet sadly gathered her things, still thinking of Mr. Sparrow's words, and headed for the door—when she heard a voice behind her.

"Scarlet?"

She turned, and saw Mr. Sparrow sitting on the edge of his desk.

"Are you okay? Usually, you're the first one to answer. Today you seemed a bit…out of it."

She was touched by his concern. He was the only teacher that ever even noticed, or cared.

"I'm fine. It's just that…" She stopped, wondering what to say. "I guess it's just that there's a lot going on for me right now. But I love the play. And I love everything you said."

He smiled back.

"I know high school can be overwhelming," he said. "So much stress at once. Especially in this year. My advice to you is to just try to focus on the work before you. Allow yourself to get lost in the text. Shakespeare's writing is four hundred years old, but if you really get lost in his stories, in his characters, you'll be surprised to see that everything he wrote about is still relevant today. We learn that others have suffered from the same things as we, for hundreds of years. We are no different. That connection to history, to others—it can help you make it through."

She thought to herself: he has no idea how right he was.

"Thank you, Mr. Sparrow. For everything," she said meaningfully, knowing this would be the last time she ever saw him again. "I just want you to know, I really enjoyed this year."

"The year is not over yet!" he said, with a smile.

"I know. I just want to say, if for some reason I don't see you again, thanks for everything."

He gave her a puzzled look, but before he could ask what she meant, she hurried from the room.

Scarlet walked into the hall and spotted Maria, closing her locker. Maria began to turn, and Scarlet hurried over to her. She figured it was now or never: she wanted to clear the air, and at least voice her side of the story.

"Maria," she said.

Slowly, reluctantly, Maria stopped and turned. She was scowling back.

"What do you want?" she snapped.

Scarlet was taken aback by her anger.

"Look, I'm really sorry about whatever it is you think happened, but I didn't steal Sage. You have to know that."

"Oh no? So what did you do exactly? He just walked away by himself?"

"It's not like that. I tried to set you two up. I really did. But he just wasn't into you."

Maria scowled, embarrassed.

"Is that what he said? Or is that what you are saying?"

"That's what he told me," Scarlet said.

But Maria just got angrier.

"Well, how could he be into me with you stealing him away? You didn't give him a chance."

"It wasn't like that. I swear," Scarlet said. "He came up to me."

"Oh, really? Like you had nothing to do with it at all?"

Scarlet felt like this was going nowhere.

"Look, I would never steal anyone out from under you," she said. "But it's not like you two were dating. You didn't even know each other. And he liked me. He approached me. I'm sorry, but that's the truth."

"You could phrase it any way you want to," Maria said. "But the bottom line is, you betrayed me. That is something I will never forgive. You were supposed to be my best friend. You were supposed to look out for me." Maria leaned forward. "We're done. I don't know you anymore."

Maria slammed her locker, and turned and marched away.

Waiting for Maria down the hall were Jasmin and Becca. They each gave Scarlet a snotty look, then turned and marched off with Maria.

Scarlet could not believe it. Maria had managed to turn her two other best friends against her. She felt like she'd been excommunicated from her group of friends. She'd never felt so alone.

As she walked, the halls felt a lot bigger, and a lot less friendly.

Scarlet spotted someone heading towards her out of the corner of her eye, and she couldn't believe it: Blake.

Oh no, Scarlet thought.

She braced herself. She could only imagine what her dad might've said to him the night before. She was already cringing with embarrassment. She was beginning to think that coming to school today had been a bad idea. Could this day get any worse?

"Hey," Blake said.

"Hey."

"So I like ran into your dad last night," he said, sounding nervous. "He like cornered me in at the party. He was pretty pissed."

"Sorry," she said. "I really am."

He shrugged.

"Whatever. He thought I was like a druggy or something. He's so got the wrong idea. Is he always like that?"

Scarlet shrugged.

"He's pretty protective, I guess."

Blake looked down and toed the floor.

"Well, like, anyway," he said, "I'm sorry that, like, you left when you did. I didn't really, like, get a chance to finish talking to you."

Scarlet looked at him.

"Actually I think you had your chance. But you let Vivian get in the way."

It was time for Scarlet to air the truth. She'd had enough of half-truths. He could either take it or leave it. She really didn't care anymore. Now, all she thought about was Sage. Blake had had his chance; he was too late.

The weird thing was, it was like Blake sensed it. He was acting differently towards her. It was like he sensed that she no longer cared—and that made him want her even more. In fact, she had never seen him seem so into her before.

"Well like listen, anyway," he continued, stumbling, "the dance tonight. I really want to take you. Will you be my date?" he asked, finally looking up and asking her directly.

Scarlet was shocked.

Now? Of all times? Why did he have to ask her now?

She thought of the irony: if he'd asked her only 48 hours before, she would have been thrilled—she would have given anything. But now, she had genuinely lost interest. Now, she had Sage. And with Sage in her life, nothing else mattered. This dance, her friends, the cliques, the fights—all of it seemed so petty to her now. It felt like a world that was already far away from her.

"I'm sorry Blake," she said. "But I can't go with you."

Blake looked at her, eyes open wide in astonishment. Clearly that was not the answer he had expected.

Scarlet didn't wait for a response. She turned and headed off, walking down the hall, thinking of Sage—and wishing the minutes would tick faster until she could see him again.

CHAPTER TWENTY

Caitlin lost all track of time and place. She had no idea how many hours she'd been in this secret back room of this rare bookstore, combing frantically through stacks and stacks of books. There were mountains of them. Worse, they were all thrown in haphazardly, in so many different positions and directions, it was almost as if someone had deliberately tried to keep them disorganized. Perhaps that was the point: perhaps whoever did this wanted to hide that book.

Caitlin had seen chaos throughout her career in bookstores and libraries—but she'd never encountered anything like this. Not only were there so many books, but they were also each so rare, so valuable. She was astonished. She'd never seen such an abundance of riches under one roof. Some of the books that she'd already passed through her hands, she knew, would be worth millions of dollars on the open market. Why had anyone treated them this way?

Clearly, Aiden knew what he was talking about when he sent her here. And now she understood why the old woman was so reluctant to open her door. She was sitting on a gold mine. Each and every one of these volumes belonged in a museum, or university library, and a part of Caitlin wanted to stop and spend time with each one as she picked it up.

But there was no time. She felt a greater urgency than ever as she rifled through one book after the next, opening the binding as quickly yet carefully as she could, glancing at the title page, skimming through it to make sure it was not a printer's error, and moving on.

Hours had passed, and she'd already managed to go through hundreds of titles. She was sneezing at a more rapid rate, the dust piling up, and was beyond exhausted, especially after not sleeping on the plane. A sense of hopelessness was starting to creep in. What if the book was not here after all? What if the page was missing? What if its ceremony didn't work? What if she didn't find it in time?

It could easily take weeks, she knew, to find the book in this room—if it even existed. She would have to get supremely lucky.

Caitlin scanned the room: there were thousands of titles yet to go, some stacked all the way to the ceiling. She swallowed, having no idea how she would even access those.

But she was not one to give up easily. She jumped back into the stacks on the floor, dealing with what she could in front of her. She rolled up her sleeves, reached over and hoisted yet another heavy volume. She went through books faster now, one, two, three at a time. Now, she just scanned the title pages and moved on. In some cases, she just scanned the spines, when visible.

After another hour or so, Caitlin, her back killing her, on her hands and knees, reached the far wall. At the very bottom of one of the tallest stacks, she yanked out one particularly large and heavy book—and as she did, the entire stack came crashing down around her; she quickly covered her head as the mountain collapsed, and got out of the way just before being completely crushed.

The books finally settled in a huge cloud of dust, and she looked up, dazed and confused. She felt like she wanted to cry.

But as she looked up, through the dust, suddenly, she spotted something that made her heart stop: the crumbled stack revealed another, smaller stack behind it, one she had not seen before. And there, right in the middle, was a book with a rich, red spine. She recognized it immediately. Suddenly, she felt an electric thrill. This was it. The matching volume.

Caitlin nearly lunged across the room, grabbing the book and holding it up to the candlelight with shaking hands.

Please God, let this be it, she thought. She pulled back the cover and nervously flipped to the title page:

De Fascino Libri Tres.

Her heart flooded with relief. She could hardly believe it. She had actually found it.

Caitlin quickly thumbed through the pages, going as fast as she could to the missing page.

Please, please be there. Please be the matching page.

She started to worry about what she would do if the matching page weren't there. Or if this was all a hoax. She was shaking with anticipation as she got closer. 530, 532....

She turned the page, and her breath stopped. There it was. 537.

And there, before her eyes, was the other half of the page.

She was speechless.

She reached into her bag and extracted the other half. She held them together. The ripped edges fit together exactly. It was a perfect match.

Hand shaking, she read the complete text for the first time. It was all in Latin, and the words lined up perfectly. She read the ritual again and again. As she did, she felt in every pore of her body that this was genuine. For the first time, her heart filled with hope. Here it was, right before her eyes. A way to save her daughter.

With a twinge of guilt, Caitlin delicately tore the half page out of the book, placing it in her folder with the other half of the page. She set the book down, picked up her bag, and hurried across the room to the stone wall, banging on it.

In seconds, it opened.

Caitlin squinted at the bright sunlight that flooded in. It was hard to believe it, but it was daytime. A bright, sunny day. Caitlin wondered how many hours she'd been in there.

The old woman stood there, staring back at her.

"You found it, didn't you?" she asked.

She stared at Caitlin meaningfully, and Caitlin suddenly realized that the old woman knew what she was after all along. How had she known? Had she been trying to hide it?

"You knew?" Caitlin asked.

The old woman stared back, expressionless.

"Why didn't you tell me where it was?" Caitlin asked.

"It's not for me to tell," the old woman said. "It's only for the worthy to find it. You, clearly, are worthy."

Caitlin's mind spun with all the implications. Had this woman been guarding a secret here? For how long? Her whole life? Who had asked her to guard it? Was she a member of some secret society? What had Caitlin stumbled into?

The old woman reached out and took Caitlin's hand with both of her small, frail hands.

"I was in your position once," she said cryptically.

Caitlin stared at her, trying to understand, wanting to know more. She wanted to know everything. But there wasn't time.

"It's real, isn't it?" Caitlin asked, fearfully. "It's all real?"

The old woman stared back.

"You will come to learn, young lady, just how real it is."

CHAPTER TWENTY ONE

Sage stood on the back terrace of the house, watching his final sunset over the Hudson River. His bags were all packed, securely in the trunk of his car, ready to go. No one had seen him pack, except his sister, the rest of his clan out and busy during the day. After their little argument, she had left him alone—going god knows where.

Sage felt bad about it. The two of them had a long and complicated relationship, about as complicated as a two-thousand-year sibling relationship could get. On the one hand, she was always his biggest critic, ready to point out his faults, and always the first one to complain to his parents about anything he did wrong. On the other hand, he always sensed that deep down she was attached to him, and truly loved him. There were, in fact, a handful of instances over the centuries when he could remember her actually standing up for him, completely surprising him. That was her: inscrutable. After two thousand years, he felt as if he still didn't really understand her.

As he looked out at the last light on the Hudson, at this place he'd called home for centuries, he felt nostalgic. He wasn't really ready to say goodbye. He wasn't ready for life to end, period. It was amazing, he realized, but despite having lived thousands of years, he still felt like he didn't have enough time. He just wanted a bit more. Just time enough to be with Scarlet, and to live out her lifetime with her.

He heard a commotion inside and took a deep breath, bracing himself. The time had come. He'd have to confront his parents. He'd have to tell them he was leaving. That this was his final goodbye.

His relationship with his parents was even more complex than his relationship with his sister. Over some of their centuries together they had felt like his parents, while over others, they had been more like siblings—and over others, they more like his own children. Their relationship seemed to be ever-evolving. Over the last hundred or so years they had fallen squarely back into the parents role, and Sage wasn't really used to it, or ready to concede to it this time. Now, when they tried to order him around, he didn't feel obliged to listen. He was through listening to them. They'd had centuries to order him around. Now, it was *his* time. Now, nobody was the boss of him. And while he knew they would throw a fit when he said his goodbyes, at the end of the day, there was really nothing they could do about it.

Sage turned and marched into the house, prepared to get it over with. He marched across the great living room, across the family room, dining room, and ascended the wide, twisting marble staircase that led to their master room. As he reached the top landing he saw the large double doors were open and walked into their thickly-carpeted room, floor to ceiling windows stretched out in a circle, overlooking the Hudson.

There, before a huge, walnut desk, sat his mother and father, both agitated, looking down, poring over papers. She wondered what paperwork they could be so upset about. After all, they would be dead in a few weeks. Didn't they realize that? They should be out there living—not sitting here worrying. He was amazed everyone spent their final weeks of mortality worrying, doing anything and everything but living. Not him. Now, finally, he was determined to live. To really live. Since meeting Scarlet, he found a reason, and he was determined to.

The two of them looked up. Immediately, their faces crumpled in frustration.

"There you are," said his father.

"Where were you all day?" asked his mother.

"I'm through with being interrogated by you both," Sage replied. "I just came to say my goodbyes. I'm leaving."

"You are not," answered his father.

"And where do you think you're going?" asked his mom.

"As I said, I'm through answering to the two of you. It's been a great two thousand years. It really has. But our time together is over. In fact, all of our time on this planet will soon be over. Let's end this graciously. Goodbyes are so cumbersome."

His parents looked at each other, then at him. They saw that he meant it. A worried look flashed across their faces.

"So that's it?" said his mom. "Just a curt goodbye? You're just going to abandon us? Abandon the whole family? Just like that?"

"That's just like you," his dad said. "Looking out for your own needs."

"This is about *her*, isn't it?" his mom asked, her eyes narrowing.

"Leave her alone," Sage said firmly. "You're wasting your time with her. Her key will do you no good if she's dead."

"On the contrary," his father corrected. "Her being dead might just do us all the good in the world. You still don't seem to realize that we will stop at nothing to have what we want, do you?"

Sage slowly shook his head. They just wouldn't listen.

"You can't harm her," he said. "Not without harming me."

His parents snorted in disdain.

"You've underestimated us, once again," his dad said. "We saw this coming—and we've already prepared our contingency plan. In fact," he said, looking down at his watch, "Lore will be leaving at any moment. He will achieve what you failed to, and will brings us what you could not get."

"And then," his mom added, "when all the rest of us achieve immortality, guess who's getting left behind?"

His parents both grinned, an evil grin, and Sage felt himself fuming. Was it true? Had they really set Lore in motion?

He studied their expressions, their small, satisfied smiles, and sensed they were telling the truth.

Sage summoned his super hearing, and zoomed in on the activity in the far reaches of the house. As he did, he could hear a commotion in a far corner of the house. He sensed Lore hurrying through the rooms. This meeting had been his signal. His parents had indeed set him in motion to find Scarlet. To kill her.

Without another word, Sage suddenly turned and raced from the room, through the open front doors, down the marble staircase. He took them three at a time, and found himself on the lower level, in the large marble foyer. At that moment, Lore was also dashing across the room, heading for the front door. Sage sensed that he was on his way to kill Scarlet. He was determined not to let that happen.

It all happened in a flash. Without thinking, Sage charged across the room and slammed into Lore, tackling him to the ground just before he reached the front door. They both slid halfway across the marble floor until they slammed into a wall.

Sage spun on top of him and pounded him several times.

But Lore was equally powerful, if not more so. He quickly spun Sage around, and kneed him hard, knocking the wind out of him.

Sage, determined, found an opening and spun and kicked Lore square in the chest, sending him across the room.

"Stop it! Both of you!" screamed Phoenicia. She ran into the room, trying to break up the two of them, as she had their entire lives.

But this time, she would not. Sage was determined. And so was Lore.

Sage thought quickly. He was desperate, absolutely desperate to stop Lore, and there was no way he could outfight him.

In a sudden flash, Sage realized what he had to do: he had to kill him. For good. For all time.

It was something Sage had wanted to do for centuries. Something that the Grand Council might even have permitted, given all the new feeding Lore had done lately. But it was something that no one in Sage's clan had the backbone to do.

But now, finally, with nothing left to lose, the time had come. It was time for Sage to kill one of his fellow Immortalists. He had never done it before. But he knew how.

As Lore got up and raced back towards Sage, this time, Sage waited. He let him get closer and closer.

Sage waited until Lore was halfway across the room, beneath a chandelier, directly across from the huge mirror over the fireplace. Then he burst into action.

Sage reached over, grabbed a candlestick from the mantle, and just as Lore was perfectly aligned with the mirror, he hurled it.

"NO!" Phoenicia screamed, realizing.

There was a huge shattering of glass, as the pieces of the mirror poured down in a million pieces. It was what Sage was aiming for. It was the only way to kill an Immortalist: to catch his reflection in a mirror, then shatter the glass.

Sage looked over, expecting to see Lore flat on his back, dying.

But what he saw stunned him.

As he looked down, he didn't see Lore there, but rather Phoenicia. She lay on the ground, gasping for air.

Out of the corner of his eye he spotted Lore dart from the house.

Sage realized what had happened: Phoenicia had jumped in the way of Lore's reflection. It was her reflection that got caught. It was she who he had killed.

Sage was suddenly overcome with guilt and grief. He had never meant to harm his sister.

"Sage?" she asked, looking up, a shocked expression on her face. "Why did you do this to me?"

"Phoenicia!" he screamed, wailing, collapsing to his knees.

He bent over her and held her head in his hands, wiping her tears away. Tears of his own dripped down onto her face.

"I'm so sorry!" he wailed. "It wasn't meant for you. It was never meant for you!"

She sat there crying, while he knelt there immobilized, unable to leave her side.

"Was she really worth it?" she asked, in a weak voice.

As she lay there, dying, Sage rocked her, her words tearing his heart in two. He knew he had to leave, to rush to the dance, to meet Scarlet. But he couldn't bring himself to run away from here, not while Phoenicia was dying like this. He knelt there and held her, wishing fate didn't have to be so cruel.

CHAPTER TWENTY TWO

Scarlet walked across the school grounds, treading through the grass on the chilly October night, sloping downhill towards the bonfire and the dance. Halloween had finally come, and she held her jacket tight around her shoulders as she went, unable to get warm.

As she walked by herself on the darkened grounds, the occasional group of kids sprinted past her dressed in costume, screaming, acting stupid. A group of boys brushed past her as they sprinted towards the bonfire and one of them shouted in her ear, acting stupid to impress his friends. She jumped, and tried to turn and shove him—but by the time she spun, he was already far ahead, racing towards the fire. She hated Halloween.

In the distance the soaring bonfire lit up the night, and it was the main source of light in the vast, open field. All around it, the school had strung up little lanterns, illuminating an area about half the size of a football field. She could already hear the music, muted, the base pulsing, and already see people dancing, wearing glow sticks around their necks, the shaking lights of their necklaces punctuating the night like small fireflies.

As she approached, she felt a growing pain in her stomach. The day had been interminably long, with her counting the minutes until it was over, until she could be done with all this and back in Sage's arms. After the disaster of her first class she'd kept a low profile, trying to just avoid everyone; she'd found an old baseball cap in her locker and had pulled it down low, sitting in the back of each class, slouching, and burying her head in her books.

But as much as she'd tried to concentrate on her books, it was no use. All she could do was think of Sage, all day long. She counted the minutes until they could leave together. She couldn't stand waiting for the night, but she knew that Sage was right, that it would be safer for them to leave town in the cover of darkness: by the time people started asking around, they would already have a head start. She also understood that he'd needed time to gather his things and say his goodbyes.

She, on the other hand, had no goodbyes left to say. After school, she'd considered going back home and packing, but didn't want to risk running into her parents. She couldn't deal with them anymore. They had become too weird and unpredictable; she almost felt as if they had turned into strangers in her house, into people she didn't even recognize. Her loving, devoted father had become angry and confrontational, and her mom had just plain lost it.

Scarlet thought back on all the happy memories they'd had together, on how much they'd loved her, how much she'd loved them, and wiped a tear from her eye. She couldn't understand how it all had gone so wrong so fast. A part of her still loved them, and missed them terribly—and wanted to go back and say goodbye to them.

But another part of her knew that would not be possible now. She was changing—she knew it, could feel it in every fiber of her being. She could feel it in her heightened senses, in her ability to hear things far away, her sense of smell, the pain in her eyes, her surges of strength and rage. Most of all, she felt it in her desire to feed, which seemed to be growing stronger each day. She could no longer lie to herself, no longer hide what was happening. She knew it was true: she was becoming a vampire.

Reading her mom's journal had convinced her. Her mom had been one, too. She felt sure of it. She didn't understand how, or when, but she knew it was true. Her mom knew. And when she saw her mom's note, that she must stop her, it was like a knife through her heart. Scarlet felt that her mom wanted her dead, and after that, she could not bear to see her mom again.

So instead of going home, Scarlet had idled the time after school down by the river, going by herself to the Hudson. She combed the shore for rocks and sea glass, throwing them into the water. She sat on a log for hours and stared out, watching the tides roll in and out, contemplating her life to come. She was internally, silently, saying goodbye to all this, to this beautiful river, to this quaint small town, to the normal life she'd once had. She knew that after tonight, after Sage picked her up, the two of them would be gone, far from here, and never coming back. And she was ready.

As she got closer to the bonfire she thought again of Sage, of their incredible night together on the island—and her heart beat faster. As upset as she was with her life, she was equally happy with Sage. He filled her heart, her entire soul, with a newfound hope. And as she thought again of what he had told her, that he only had weeks to live, she felt determined to spend every last minute with him. She was also determined to find a solution for him to live longer.

She reached down and felt her necklace, at the base of her throat, as she walked more quickly towards the fire, so close now that the voices in the crowd filled the air. She also reached down and felt the ring Sage had given her. She loved wearing it: it was like wearing a part of him. She wondered where they would go together. She didn't really care. She just wanted to get away from both their families, from all their friends, from all the obstacles in the path of their love together. She just wanted to go someplace where it could be just the two of them, with the world to themselves.

As she finally reached the big dance, Scarlet snapped out of it, and felt a swirl of emotions race through her. The day had finally come, and ironically, here she was, showing up without a date, something she'd vowed she'd never do. Not to mention that just days ago, she and Maria had vowed that if they didn't have dates, then they would go together. How quickly everything had changed. Now, here she was, alone, not even speaking to Maria; now, none of her friends were even speaking to her. Just a few days she had so desperately wanted to go with Blake, but now, she had turned him down. Now, she had a date of her own—even if he wasn't actually here yet.

As Scarlet reached the crowd, she scanned the faces, looking hopefully for any sign of Sage. She wandered through the thick crowd, looking over the hundreds of eyes. Most of the crowd were in costume, making spotting him difficult. She wondered if he'd be in costume, too—but then quickly discounted that. Of course he wouldn't. He didn't need to be: he was already different than everyone else. He was an Immortalist.

Scarlet looked down and suddenly felt self-conscious about not being in costume herself—but then realized that was silly, especially as several girls passed her dressed in vampire outfits. After all, she, Scarlet, was the real vampire here. What need did she have for a costume?

Scarlet passed folding tables on which sat huge bowls of punch, with serving ladles and cups. She noticed a few kids spiking their glasses with a clear liquid from a flask hidden in their pockets. She realized that many of these kids were probably already drunk, despite the watchful eyes of the school administration.

The music was blaring, blasting a dance song. On the makeshift dance floor in the grass, hundreds of kids were dancing to the beat; it was a strange sight to see this dance club outside, on a football field. She kept working her way through the crowd, winding between groups of people, looking at all the costumes, wondering if behind any of them was Sage.

She felt increasingly desperate as she reached the end of the crowd and saw no sign of him. She flooded with panic as worst-case scenarios crossed her mind: had he changed his mind? Would he not show, leave her stranded? Would she be left all alone in the world?

The thought set her heart pounding. She quickly tried to push it out of her mind.

Stay positive, she told herself, again and again. *Maybe he's just late.*

She circled through the crowd again, and came to the huge bonfire. Dozens of kids stood around it, staring at the flames. Most of these were the kids without dates, not dancing on the floor. A lot of them had long sticks, roasting marshmallows. The huge pile of wood burned higher and higher into the night, crackling and popping as it did.

As Scarlet scanned the faces, she suddenly recognized a familiar face: Maria.

Maria noticed Scarlet at the same time. She looked at her, then rolled her eyes and turned and walked away.

It hurt Scarlet, and made her want to try one more time to talk sense to her former friend. Maybe now she'd be ready to listen. She hated leaving things like this.

Scarlet hurried over to her and grabbed her arm as she was walked away.

"Maria, wait!"

Maria turned, and stared back coldly.

"What do you want?" she spat. "Where's your boyfriend? Did he dump you already?"

Scarlet was taken aback by her nastiness. She hardly knew how to respond.

"You don't have to be mean," Scarlet said. "Like I said, I didn't do anything."

Maris stared back, seething, and Scarlet could see she had not forgiven her.

"And like I said, we're over," Maria said.

Maria turned and stormed off into the crowd. Not far away were Jasmin and Becca; they stared back at Scarlet as if she were their enemy now, too. As Maria reached them, the whole group turned their backs as one, and disappeared into the crowd.

Just as Scarlet was feeling worse than ever, she felt a tapping on her shoulder.

Her heart swelled, as she hoped and prayed it was Sage, here to rescue her from all this.

But she was crushed to see it wasn't him. It was Blake. He stood there, smiling nervously back at her. His eyes looked bloodshot, and she could smell vodka on his breath.

"I saw you standing here alone," he said. "Does that mean you don't have a date?"

Scarlet hardly knew how to respond. She really did not want to get into it with him now. She was over him.

"I…um…yes…I do."

Blake raised his eyebrows in surprise, and then she saw a small smile at the corner of his lips, as if he didn't believe her.

"Well, where is he?" he asked.

She scanned the crowd, searching again for Sage, willing him to appear.

But again, she saw no sign of him. Her heart fell. She couldn't understand it. What could possibly have happened? She felt even worse than ever, as if the universe were rubbing it in.

"I don't know," she finally answered, truthfully.

"Doesn't sound like a good date to me," Blake said. "I don't have a date either," he added. "Vivian actually asked me. Can you believe it? That was bold."

"What did you say?" Scarlet asked.

"I said no," he said, a serious look in his eyes. "Because I wanted to go with you. And I was hoping maybe you'd show."

He said it with such sincerity, that for a moment, Scarlet felt herself looking into his eyes, remembering why she liked him in the first place.

She quickly looked away.

"Look, Scarlet, I know I've been a jerk," he said. "I'm really sorry. I was thinking about everything you said. About not standing up for you, in front of Vivian. And you're right. I should have. I'm sorry. It was stupid. Anyway, the thing is, I know how I feel now. I guess I was just confused, ya know? But anyway, I really want to be with you. I really want you to be my girlfriend. You don't have to give me an answer now. But just think about it, okay? I promise, I'll change."

Scarlet stood there, not knowing what to say. He seemed so sincere, his words at least took the edge off of her anger and upset towards him.

"Thank you for saying all that," she said. "I appreciate it."

"I'm going to get a drink," he said. "I'll come back in a little bit. If your friend still isn't here, maybe we can dance?"

She doubted very much she'd be standing here when he got back. If Sage didn't show, she was leaving. But she appreciated it anyway.

Blake disappeared back into the crowd, and she sighed and turned the other way, deciding to get away from Blake and patrol the other side of the field. Maybe Sage was waiting in the far corners, lurking in the shadows.

As she made it halfway, suddenly she heard a voice.

"Well, if it isn't miss congeniality."

Scarlet's heart sank. She stopped and slowly turned, and there, behind her, stood Vivian, flanked by all of her friends. They stared down at her with mean smiles, and she could tell by their glossy eyes that they were all drunk. She could also see immediately how mad Vivian was at being here without a date. Clearly, that must have embarrassed her, and she was looking to take it on someone. She had finally found her target.

"So you think you can just throw beer on me at a party and get away with it?" Vivian asked.

"I never threw beer on you," Scarlet responded.

"No, but your little friend did," she answered. "On your behalf."

"I can't control what my friends do."

"But you wanted her to, didn't you? And she did it for you."

Scarlet was in no mood for this. She really didn't want a confrontation. Not now. Not here.

She turned and began to walk away.

Suddenly, she felt a hand digging into her shoulder, nails digging into her skin. She was yanked around as Vivian spun her around.

"Don't you ever turn your back on me!" Vivian snapped.

Vivian reached back to smack Scarlet hard across the face, and as she did, something suddenly overtook Scarlet. It was like her senses went into overdrive, by themselves. She saw Vivian's hand coming at her in slow-motion, and everything slowed down around her. She reached out, her reflexes a thousand times faster than she ever thought possible, and easily caught Vivian's wrist.

Scarlet stood there, holding it. She squeezed and squeezed, and felt superhuman strength rush through her.

Vivian dropped to her knees, crying out in pain.

"Let go of me!" she screamed.

Suddenly, one of Vivian's friends charged Scarlet, and as she did, Scarlet leaned back and kicked her in the solo plexus. The kick was so powerful, it sent her flying back like a torpedo, into all her other friends, sending them all crashing to the ground.

That caused a big stir in the crowd, and several people turned and looked their way, causing a commotion. Scarlet stood there, rage coursing through her, as she stared down at Vivian.

Vivian looked up at her, wide-eyed, eyes filled with fear, shaking.

As Scarlet stared down at her, something else overwhelmed her. She felt blood rushing up through her face, felt it beginning to transform, felt her two incisor teeth lengthening. She felt a tingling on her lips.

She snarled down at Vivian, and it was an unnerving, animal-like noise that startled even her.

Vivian's eyes opened twice as wide.

"What are you?" Vivian asked.

Scarlet was overcome by an insatiable desire to feed. Every pore in her body screamed out for blood—for Vivian's blood. Her body was positively quaking. She was dying to kneel down and sink her teeth into Vivian's throat. She saw herself drinking and drinking, filling up on her blood. It was a craving so strong, she didn't know if she could stop it.

"Scarlet!" came a harsh voice from behind.

There was something in that voice, something just strong enough, to make Scarlet turn.

There stood Lore. He stood out in the crowd, wearing his tight leather jacket, towering over everyone.

Scarlet turned back and backhanded Vivian, smacking her so hard, the sound rippled through the crowd.

Vivian collapsed, face first, in the grass, and the crowd gasped as she did.

Scarlet turned and walked over to Lore.

"Where is Sage?" she snapped, her voice still deep and dark from the transformation.

Lore smiled, slowly shaking his head.

"He's not coming," he said. "He told me to bring you a message. Sorry. He changed his mind."

Scarlet felt a knife plunged into her heart at the words. She had never felt so betrayed. She felt completely crushed.

"He also asked me to tell you to give me the necklace," Lore said, reaching out a hand.

Scarlet stared down, and suddenly realized Lore was lying. Sage would never tell him to ask for the necklace. Or would he?

"Go to hell," Scarlet snarled.

Slowly, Lore's smile dropped, as his face contorted with rage. Before her eyes, she watched him transform, into a huge, raven-like creature. His wings spread wider and wider as he stepped forward to wrap them around Scarlet.

"I can kill you," he snarled. "And I will kill you."

"Then kill me," she snarled back. "You're not the only one who is immortal."

Lore leapt into motion, bringing his wings down as if to smother her.

But suddenly, Lore's wings stopped in mid-air, just inches away from her. He looked down at her ring, and his eyes opened wide in astonishment.

"He gave you the ring," he hissed, trembling, frozen.

Scarlet leaned back and kicked Lore hard in the chest, so hard, she sent him flying, hundreds of feet, across the entire field, into its darkest corners.

She'd had enough. She suddenly felt certain Sage would never come, and felt her heart breaking into a million little pieces. She knew that she couldn't stay in this crowd any longer: another minute here, and she would start feeding on everyone in sight.

So instead, with a final snarl and roar of anguish, Scarlet burst out of there, sprinting away from the field, from the school, from the dance—far, far away from everything, and deep into the darkest depths of the night.

CHAPTER TWENTY THREE

Caitlin burst through the front door of her house, and right into Caleb's waiting arms. He hugged her tight, and it felt so good to be back in his grip. Ruth stood by her side, whining and barking, leaping up on her.

"I'm sorry," he said. "I'm so sorry for not believing you."

Caitlin hugged him back, not wanting to let him go either, especially after all the darkness they'd been through. Finally, she felt vindicated. Finally, he believed her. She felt his love for her coursing through, and as she did, she felt rejuvenated, restored, no longer so alone in the world. Finally, she felt as if she had a partner to help her deal with all this, to help save their daughter.

All was right in the world again. Here was Caleb, back to his old self, at her side, trusting her, believing in her. Finally, he realized she wasn't crazy. Finally, he realized she'd been right all along—realized that their daughter was, in fact, turning into a vampire.

It had all happened so quickly, ever since Caitlin had landed back on American soil. She had called Caleb the second her plane touched down, and they'd been talking on the phone ever since, all during her drive back from the airport. She had eagerly filled him in, and was relieved and surprised that he was not only eager to hear it all this time, but that he actually believed her.

He had surprised her with his own tale of what had happened between he and Scarlet, of how she had snarled and thrown him across the room. He realized that no human could have done that, and finally realized that she was not the Scarlet they both knew. Now, he wanted Caitlin's help. Now, he wanted to hear everything.

Caitlin, in turn, had filled him in on all the details of her search, on her journal, her meeting with Aiden, her research in her library, and her discovery in the Paris bookstore. She told him about the missing page. The ritual. She told him how urgent it was that they find Scarlet and perform it, before it was too late.

But Caitlin's heart sank as Caleb told her Scarlet had left the previous night and he hadn't been able to find her since. He'd been trying her cell for hours, and had called all her friends again, and had been unable to get through to anyone. He'd also called the cops. He said he had a wide net out looking for her, but nothing yet. He was more panic-stricken than he'd ever been.

Caitlin's mind swarmed with the possibilities, and she felt a greater urgency than ever to find her.

She pulled back and looked at him.

"Have you heard anything at all? Anything?" she asked.

He shook his head, disappointedly.

"All I have is a text from one of her friends. She said she thought she saw her at the school dance. And that she saw her leave. Alone. That was about an hour ago."

"Where would she have gone?" Caitlin asked.

"I have no idea." He looked at her. "That ritual. Do you really think it's authentic?" he asked.

Caitlin reached into her bag and pulled out the folder. She extracted the delicate halves of the paper, lining them up on the table before them.

Caleb looked down and examined them, and his eyes opened wide in surprise.

"It looks ancient," he said. "What language is that?"

"Latin," she said. "But it won't do us any good if we don't find her—soon."

Caitlin's cell suddenly lit up, and her heart skipped a beat, praying it was Scarlet.

But then she looked down and was crestfallen to see it was just Polly.

"Polly, what's up?" she asked curtly. "Have you heard anything?"

"Listen," Polly said excitedly, "I was able to get through on text to a friend of hers, who texted a friend of hers, who answered back and said she knew how to find Scarlet."

"How?" Caitlin asked excitedly, as Caleb crowded in.

"Apparently, Scarlet has an app called Loopt. A lot of these kids have it these days. If you're logged in, it lets you track your friends via GPS. And her friend's logged in and says she saw Scarlet's logged in, too. She might have logged in manually or she might have not turned off her settings to be logged in by default."

"Wait a second," Caitlin said, trying to understand as Polly spoke so fast. "What does this mean?"

"I'm saying we can track her phone. We don't know if she has her phone or if someone stole it, of course, but at least we can get to the phone. At least until the battery dies or it powers off. We have to hurry."

Caitlin's heart skipped a beat in anticipation.

"Where is her phone right now?" Caitlin asked. She prayed it wasn't someplace dangerous.

"The app shows her on Route 99. About 3 miles south of town. At a roadside bar. Pete's."

Caitlin's was panic stricken. Scarlet? At Pete's? What on earth would she be doing there? That place was a gross little roadside bar in a bad part of town, in a trailer park about a mile down the road from the local jail. It was a haven for freshly-released convicts, looking for their first drink out. It was a place where the worse misfits gathered, a place you didn't even slow for when you zoomed by it on the highway. Scarlet's being there could only mean danger. Real danger.

"Pick us up on the way," Polly said. "We'll track her."

"We're on our way," Caitlin said.

Caleb was already in motion, heading for the door, and within moments he had the car started and Caitlin jumped in. He peeled out and they took off down the quiet side streets, blowing stop signs, doing 80 miles an hour. They would stop at nothing until they found her.

CHAPTER TWENTY FOUR

Kyle stepped through the open gates of the prison and took his first step to the outside world, as the gates slammed close behind him. They slammed them extra hard, Kyle realized, as if wanting to rattle him, to take away his joy. It was the final insult of this merciless institution, of these sadistic guards, who had done everything to break him over the last five years.

But he wasn't going to let anything bother him now. Now, for the first time in as long as he could remember, he was on the other side of these gates, on the other side of the barbed-wire tower. Now, for the first time, he didn't have to answer to these cretins. He was a free man. Free. He could hardly believe it.

Kyle grinned from ear to ear, breathing in the crisp October air, relishing what it felt like to be outside. It was amazing not to have to hear his fellow convicts screaming and hollering reverberating all around him, all the time. To not have to fear for his life. And most of all, he thought, as he turned slowly and glared at the guards behind him, not have to answer to anyone. Least of all these pigs.

Kyle grinned wide as he slowly raised his middle finger right at the guard standing a few feet from him, close to the gate.

In the past, this guard would've taken his baton and beaten Kyle down, thrown him in isolation. But now, there wasn't a thing the guard could do. Now Kyle was a free man, an upstanding citizen, just like anybody else.

Well, maybe not so upstanding. But then again, Kyle never had been. From the time he was young, he had taken a pleasure in torturing small animals, in bullying his classmates, in beating anyone younger than him. It had all stemmed, the shrinks told him, from his abusive father, who had beaten Kyle so badly and for so long that one day, when Kyle finally grew big and strong enough, he beat this dad back. That was the day his dad left—and he had never seen him again.

But by then, the damage had been done. Kyle had been 16, already huge for a boy his size, six foot five with shoulders as broad as a tree trunk, and hardened enough to beat his six foot father to a pulp. After that moment, Kyle had never looked back. The 16 years of taking a beating had infused in him an insatiable rage. He had to let it out on the world.

Everywhere he'd looked, he'd seen a target. Highly paranoid and over-sensitive, he imagined people were staring back at him, insulting him, ready to abuse him in the same way his father had. And he lashed out. He beat others up before they could get anywhere near him, whether they deserved it or not. He left quite a trail, and by the time he reached 19, he'd already been in and out of dozens of juvenile detention centers.

Now, at 35, Kyle was a hardened convict. He'd spent more of his life behind bars than outside them, and true to form, he was already dreaming of his next crime. The next store he could rob. The next cop he could beat down. The next girl he could attack. The next bar fight he could get into. His need for violence was insatiable—and the last five years had only hardened it.

The way Kyle saw it, he was only 35, and he still had at least another 30 good years ahead of him of causing hell. When he reached 65, he figured, if he wasn't dead, he'd retire, or find a way to go out with a bang. Too bad there was no pension plan for criminals, he thought.

Kyle began to head down the gravel road, a new bounce to his step, kicking up dirt as he went. He got onto the busy Route 99, and walked along its shoulder. Cars whizzed by and as they did, he grinned and stuck out a thumb. Of course, as the headlights lit up his scarred face, reflected off his bald head, no one dared stop.

But that just made him grin wider. He wouldn't have stopped for himself either. No one was that stupid.

Kyle didn't really want a ride anyway. He just enjoyed scaring others. Maybe he'd strike just a little bit of panic in some driver's heart, maybe in the heart of some mom or her kids. He grinned wider at the thought, sneering at a Volkswagen Beetle as it sped by.

His real destination was just down the road, a little dive bar that he remembered from years ago. It was the perfect spot to get a drink and kick off his hell raising. Maybe he could beat the hell out of a few unsuspecting locals—and maybe, if he got lucky, top it off by finding some girls to take advantage of.

Pete's. That was its name.

CHAPTER TWENTY FIVE

Scarlet walked by herself down Route 99, cars whizzing past her, and never felt more alone. It had been the worst day she could remember.

She ran over and over in her mind what could have possibly happened to Sage. How could he have abandoned her like that? Had he changed his mind? Was it something she'd said? Had he realized that he was just not that into her all along? Had he decided to stay with his family instead? Had it all just been a lie? Had he really sent his cousin for the necklace?

The thought of him broke her heart completely. Sage was the last person in the world who she thought would let her down. Now, after the fights with her parents and her friends, she felt she had no one—absolutely no one—left to turn to. All the joy and optimism that had swelled her heart this morning now came crashing down, sending her lower than she had ever been. She truly felt she had nothing left to live for.

Scarlet walked with her head down, dejected, barely even noticing the cars. She felt, inside her, something slowly stirring, welling up. It was a slow, simmering rage, something unsatisfied, something that needed to be fulfilled. It was a desire to take revenge on something. On someone. A desire to feed. She felt her skin itching, all her senses on edge, like, she imagined, a drug addict probably felt when needing a hit. Previously, she had been able to keep it all in check. But now, she couldn't hold it back anymore. More and more, she felt as if she were about to explode. She had a sinking feeling that once she found her next target, she'd be unable to control herself.

A part of her wanted to run, to get away, to avoid mankind. But another part of her was feeling this unquenchable desire that had to be sated. Her veins were alive, burning inside of her. She needed fresh blood to fill them.

Suddenly, a car screeched to a stop right in front of her, snapping her out of it. She looked up and saw a beat-up black pickup truck. In the cab sat two men, mid 30s. They backed up, until they were right beside her, slammed on the brakes, and peered out.

She saw beer cans in their hands, and could smell stale beer coming from inside the cab; she could see from their faces that they were drunk. They were unshaven, ugly men; their hands were covered in grease, and they looked like they hadn't changed in weeks.

"Hey little girl," came the slurred voice of the man in the passenger seat. "What ya doing on a road like this all by herself so late at night?"

"Jump in and we'll give you a ride!" the driver yelled out.

"We'll take you for a good time," the other one added.

Scarlet felt her rage rising, nearly uncontrollable. She zoomed in on the pulses in their throats, watched their heartbeats.

With a supreme force of will, she forced herself to look away. She turned and continued walking down the highway, ignoring them.

"Hey girl I'm talking to you!" one of them shouted.

A second later, she heard the door to the truck open and close, heard boots on the gravel, and heard the sound of them both rushing up to her. She sensed that in just a moment, one of them would grab her, probably try to throw her into the car and take her who knows where.

But they picked the wrong girl, at the wrong time.

At the last second Scarlet spun, just as the first one was about to grab her. She snarled, her fangs protruding, and an unearthly noise filled the air.

The two men stopped cold in their tracks, shocked, eyes opened wide in fear.

In that moment, Scarlet felt she could easily plunge her fangs into their throats, feed—and she wanted to more than anything.

But with another supreme effort, she forced herself not to.

Instead, she grabbed the closest one by his plaid shirt, picked him up high over her head, and leaned back and threw him.

He went flying, smashing through the windshield, landing in the front seat, shattering glass all over the place.

The other man peed his pants. Eyes open wide in terror, he turned and sprinted and ran back into the truck. He jumped in and peeled out of there. Within moments, their red tail lights were a dot on the horizon.

Scarlet looked around, breathing hard, and took several deep breaths.

Slowly, she willed herself back to normal, and slowly, her fangs retracted. She was proud of her self-discipline.

But she felt like a starving animal. She didn't know how much longer she could take it.

She scanned the horizon, and saw, not far from her, a roadside bar. It had a cheap, flashing neon sign, missing a letter. It blinked: Pete's.

She was dying of thirst. Maybe if she had some water, some food—anything—it might taper off her craving. She had to try something. Anything.

Pete's it was.

CHAPTER TWENTY SIX

As Scarlet walked through the door of the small dive bar, she knew right away that it was a mistake. A dozen or so locals sat slumped over the bar, big burly men, and they all turned and stared as the door closed behind her.

The bartender looked up, too, as if wondering what a girl like her was doing in a place like this. It was a disgusting little place, fluorescent lights flashing, a broken pinball machine off to one side, a small pool table missing balls. The bar looked more like a living room than a bona fide establishment. It was late, she realized, and clearly these men were deep into their drinking. She could sense the dark energy, and a part of her wanted to turn and run.

But another part of her was desperate. She needed water, food— she didn't know what. Something was happening to her body, and she could hardly think straight.

Scarlet rushed to the bar, breathing hard, and flagged down the bartender.

"Water," she gasped. "I need water. Please."

He warily filled a glass with tap water and handed it to her.

"You got ID to be in here?" he asked.

Without pausing, Scarlet chugged the entire 16 ounce glass of water. It felt so good going down her throat. She was parched, and didn't know why.

"More," she gasped.

The bartended filled up her glass, and she chugged it again.

She took a deep breath, and felt a little better. But she still didn't feel sated. Her veins were still screaming for something else. Something more.

Blood.

Scarlet turned and scanned the faces of the men at the bar, who all leered back at her as if she were a thing of prey. They licked their lips, as if waiting to pounce.

Suddenly there was the distinct sound of a bolt sliding shut; Scarlet turned and saw a huge man standing at the door. He had just finished locking it, and he blocked the exit with his massive frame. He stared at Scarlet as if manna from heaven had just fallen into his lap.

Scarlet willed herself to breathe, to stay calm. She didn't want to hurt these men. She didn't want to kill them. She didn't want to feed on anyone. All she wanted was to be left alone. To get out of here. To let this nightmare end.

The huge man, his face covered in scars and with a shining, bald head, walked right up to her. He sneered down at her. He was the biggest cretin she had ever seen.

"My name is Kyle," he said to her, as he approached. "What's yours, little girl?"

"Go to hell," Scarlet said.

A chorus of oohs arose from the bar, as the other men roared in amusement.

Kyle's, humiliated, turned beet-red.

He reached down with both hands and grabbed her wrists and yanked her to him. In the same motion, he reached around and picked her up off the floor and carried her off, as if she were a ragdoll.

Scarlet struggled and kicked and elbowed, but it did no good. This man was huge, as strong as a rock, and she couldn't wiggle free. She summoned her rage, her supernatural strength, to come—but for some reason it would not.

"Get your hands off of me!" she screamed.

"Honey," he said, as he dragged her behind the bar, through a hidden door, into a secluded back room, "that's the last thing I am going to do to you tonight."

The final thing Scarlet saw was the door slamming behind her, as the man held her tighter and carried her deeper, and deeper, into the blackness.

CHAPTER TWENTY SEVEN

Caitlin sat in the passenger seat while Caleb floored their car, Sam and Polly in the back. They had picked them up on the way and Polly was tracking Scarlet's movements on her iphone. They all sped down Route 99, each on edge, Caleb doing 100 miles an hour as he raced for Pete's.

"I see her blue dot!" Polly yelled out, glued to her phone. "She's still there. We're getting closer. I see it!"

"I hope it's really her, not just her phone," Caitlin said, with a sinking feeling.

For the millionth time, she agonized over what her daughter could be doing at Pete's. She wondered again if she'd made a mistake to leave for so long, to go to Paris, if she should've stayed here, at home, and done whatever she could to protect her. She felt overwhelmed with waves of guilt and anxiety.

But she at least took comfort in being here with Caleb and Polly and Sam. It would be a rough crowd at Pete's, and if there were any altercations, there was no one she'd rather have there than Caleb and Sam. Between the two of them, they'd have the muscle they needed to get Scarlet out of anything.

"THERE!" Caitlin screamed, pointing. "Up there, on the right!"

Caleb dramatically slowed the car, bringing it down to 40, and made a hard turn off the road, onto the gravel parking lot of Pete's. A truck's air-horn, behind him, blared at him as he did, but he didn't care.

They screeched to a stop right in front of the bar.

"She's in here!" Polly screamed. "For sure!"

The second they pulled up, the four of them jumped out of the car, the engine barely off, and raced as one for the door. Caleb reached it first, Sam right behind them, and Caleb tried the knob.

"It's locked," he said, confused.

"That makes no sense," Caitlin said. "The lights are on. I see people in there. I hear music."

"I'm telling you, they locked it," he said.

"Why would they do that?" Polly asked.

And then, suddenly, with a pit in her stomach, Caitlin realized. They wanted to keep somebody locked in. Her stomach dropped further, as she thought of Scarlet. Was she being held captive in there?

"Stand back," Caleb said. He must have been thinking the same thing.

He took a running start, and put a shoulder to the door. It shook, but didn't give.

"I'll help," Sam said, stepping up. "On three, we ram this thing. ONE…TWO…THREE!"

The two of them took a few steps and rammed their shoulders into the door, which went flying open in a splintering of wood.

The two of them went flying inside, Caitlin and Polly on their heels. As they did, it was immediate mayhem.

A crowd of about a dozen locals, big, burly men, scowled back. There was an excited energy in the air, as if they were all up to something—or hiding something.

"What the hell do you think you're doing to our door?" one of them screamed.

"Who the hell you think you are?" another yelled.

"Where is she?" Caleb screamed back, walking towards them. "My daughter. WHERE IS SHE?"

The locals grinned to each other, and as they did, Caitlin knew immediately that she was here.

"You mean that sweet little thing?" one of them mocked. "I'd say she's rounding second base right about now!"

There followed a chorus of laughter from the other locals.

Caleb's face turned a shade of purple, as he took on a darker expression than Caitlin had ever seen in her life.

He charged the local who spoke, grabbed him with both hands, heaved him high above his head, and threw him into his friend. The two of them collapsed onto the floor.

There was a shattering of glass, as another local snuck up on Caleb from behind and, before anyone could react, smashed him hard with a bottle on the back of his head.

Caitlin watched, horrified, as Caleb sank to the ground.

"Oh my god, Caleb!" she yelled.

Sam jumped into action. He tackled the local, driving him down to the ground.

But a moment later, three more locals jumped on top of Sam, kicking him in his exposed rib cage and back, and beating him down.

Caitlin ran to the bar, grabbed an empty bottle and ran over and smashed the man on the back of the head who was kicking Sam.

But suddenly, she found herself back-handed hard across the face. She was then shoved against a wall, as another man grabbed her from behind, restraining her arms. Another man grabbed Polly.

Caitlin stood there, pinned, helpless as she watched Caleb lying there unconscious, and Sam getting beaten to a pulp on the ground.

God only knew where Scarlet was. This was the most horrifying moment of Caitlin's life. She would do anything, anything, just to break free, to be able to save her husband, her brother, her best friend—and most of all, her daughter—from these disgusting locals.

She wondered if the locals would kill them all. It certainly seemed like it was going that way. She felt more helpless than she ever had.

That was when the door to the bar burst open.

The locals turned, and Caitlin saw, standing there, a boy who looked maybe 18. He was tall, with broad shoulders, striking gray eyes, and a proud, noble chin. He wore a tight leather jacket, and she had the strangest feeling that she'd met him before.

Caitlin wasn't exactly sure what happened next. She blinked, and a moment later, the boy was across the room. She didn't understand how he covered so much ground so quickly. But he did. And in another blink of an eye, he had already managed to knock out all five people who were kicking Sam. He punched and kicked in such a whirlwind, it was as if a tornado entered the room.

Caitlin watched, wide-eyed, in awe. Inspired by him, she raised her elbow and brought it back, elbowing the man holding her hard in the solo plexus. He keeled over, and she reached around, grabbed a bottle and smashed it hard across his face. He collapsed to his knees and she kicked him hard in the gut several times.

The boy circled the room, knocking out everyone except for Caleb and Sam and Caitlin and Polly. Within a moment, the floor was littered with bodies. She wondered who this boy was? How he had this strength? And why he was helping them?

The boy rushed over and helped Caleb and Sam to their feet. The two of them looked at him, dazed, not understanding what had happened.

"Thank you," Caitlin said, stepping forward. "You saved our lives. Who are you?"

"Sage. Where is she?"

Caitlin wondered how he knew about Scarlet. Had he come here looking for her?

The boy didn't wait for a response. He searched the room, then his eyes locked on the door behind the bar.

He rushed it, and Caitlin and the others rushed it, too, right behind him.

Without pausing, Sage kicked the door down, and it went flying off its hinges.

Caitlin stopped in her tracks, horrified: she could not believe what she saw.

*

Although Scarlet struggled, she could not overpower the man. He had carried her into this back room, turned on the cheap fluorescent light, and had thrown her across the room; she'd landed hard on the firm, cheap couch, banging her head on the wood frame. She lay there, shaking, trying to get her bearings. As she sat up, he backhanded her hard across the face, knocking her down.

The man walked across the room, turning on another lamp on the far side.

"I want to be able to see you when I do this," he snarled. "Looks like it's my lucky night."

Scarlet lay there, burning with the injustice of the world. It wasn't fair. It just wasn't fair.

She started to experience a new sensation. An anger rose up through her, a deep, primal anger at the world. It overwhelmed her, took over her, rose up through her veins. Up until now, she had tried so hard to hold back her urge not to hurt anyone. Not to feed on anyone. It was so against her nature.

But as this disgusting man, this awful predator, walked towards her, looming so large, Scarlet could not hold back any longer. The primal rage rose up through her—and this time, she let it rise. A tremendous heat prickled in her veins, raised her hairs, made them stand on end, from her toes up to her head.

154

She breathed harder, and heavier, and slowly, she felt her fangs protrude. She felt transformed. No longer was she afraid of her anger. Of her desire. Now she was ready to embrace it. Now, finally, she was ready to embrace who she was. Ready to feed. Ready to destroy.

As the man came closer, now just a few feet away, Scarlet suddenly jumped to her feet. She stood there opposite him, and as she did, she let out a unearthly, horrific snarl. It was the anguished cry of a wild beast, caged for centuries, finally let loose. Her chains had finally been unbound.

Despite the man's huge height and strength and breadth, despite his scars, despite his being the meanest man she'd ever met, he stopped cold in his tracks at the sight of her. And in his eyes, she could see, for the first time, real terror. He was panic stricken. In a state of total shock.

But it was too late for him now. Any ounce of compassion within her had left long ago. This was the new Scarlet. Now, it was her against the world.

Scarlet lunged for the man, leaned her head back, and plunged her fangs deep into his throat.

They sank deeper and deeper, hitting his vein.

He shrieked, as he collapsed to his knees.

She drank.

She drank and drank and drank, as the man collapsed to the ground beneath her. She pinned him down, like an animal, on top of him, and as she did, she sucked out every last ounce of his blood.

She felt her body infusing with a new kind of energy, a boundless, limitless power. For the first time, her craving felt relieved. She felt restored, rejuvenated, satisfied in a way that she hadn't been able to be satisfied since this all began. Finally, she felt whole.

At that moment, the door burst open.

She turned, startled, and lifted her bloody fangs.

Through her bloody, red haze, dimly, she saw figures she recognized. She saw five people, standing there, looking down at her—and somewhere, deep in her consciousness, she remembered them. Her parents. Her aunt and uncle. Sage.

But that was all hazy, a distant memory now. Now, they were just figures in a haze. Figures she barely knew.

For Scarlet had transformed. She was no longer a teenager. No longer a human.

She was now a vampire. A full-fledged vampire, ready to feed on the world.

And without another moment's hesitation, she turned, and burst through the back window.

She burst out into the full, moonlit night, roaring as she did, bounding off into the universe, ready to go anywhere, far from here.

And willing to stop at nothing until she found her next kill.

Books by Morgan Rice

THE SORCERER'S RING
A QUEST OF HEROES (BOOK #1)
A MARCH OF KINGS (BOOK #2)
A FEAST OF DRAGONS (BOOK #3)
A CLASH OF HONOR (BOOK #4)
A VOW OF GLORY (BOOK #5)
A CHARGE OF VALOR (BOOK #6)
A RITE OF SWORDS (BOOK #7)
A GRANT OF ARMS (BOOK #8)
A SKY OF SPELLS (BOOK #9)
A SEA OF SHIELDS (BOOK #10)
A REIGN OF STEEL (BOOK #11)

THE SURVIVAL TRILOGY
ARENA ONE (Book #1)
ARENA TWO (Book #2)

the Vampire Journals
turned (book #1)
loved (book #2)
betrayed (book #3)
destined (book #4)
desired (book #5)
betrothed (book #6)
vowed (book #7)
found (book #8)
resurrected (book #9)
craved (book #10)